"I was at my doctor's this morning," Dodi told him, her voice raspier than usual.

"And? What's the problem? Are you ill?"

Was that a hint of worry she heard in Jago's growly voice or was she imagining it? No, he was just frustrated she was wasting his precious time.

Annoyed at him and irritated at herself, she lifted her head to see him leaning his butt against the edge of the desk, his feet crossed at the ankles. His suit pants brushed her bare knee and she wished she could touch him, just to anchor herself as she delivered her conversational hand grenade.

She could put this off and tell him later...

No, she had to tell him some time and it might as well be now. Dodi pulled in a deep breath, forced her eyes to his face and rubbed the back of her neck.

"I'm pregnant. And the baby is yours."

Scandals of the Le Roux Wedding

Will the bride say "I do"?

Thadie Le Roux's society wedding is set to be the biggest and most lavish South Africa has ever seen! Her twin billionaire brothers, Jago and Micah, will spare no expense, because family is everything *and* they have the Le Roux name to uphold.

And that certainly helps when things start to go wrong! A scathing social media campaign here, a canceled venue there... Will Thadie ever make it down the aisle? Not least considering all the Le Rouxs are about to discover that for a union to be binding, it must first be forged in red-hot attraction!

Read Jago and Dodi's story in
The Billionaire's One-Night Baby
Available now!

Look out for Micah's and Thadie's stories
Coming soon!

Joss Wood

THE BILLIONAIRE'S ONE-NIGHT BABY

ISBN-13: 978-1-335-56867-0

The Billionaire's One-Night Baby

For questions and comments about the quality of this book, please contact us at CustomerService@Harlequin.com.

Harlequin Enterprises ULC
22 Adelaide St. West, 41st Floor
Toronto, Ontario M5H 4E3, Canada
www.Harlequin.com

Printed in U.S.A.

Joss Wood loves books and traveling—especially to the wild places of southern Africa and, well, anywhere. She's a wife, a mom to two teenagers and a slave to two cats. After a career in local economic development, she now writes full-time. Joss is a member of Romance Writers of America and Romance Writers of South Africa.

Books by Joss Wood

Harlequin Presents

The Rules of Their Red-Hot Reunion

South Africa's Scandalous Billionaires

How to Undo the Proud Billionaire
How to Win the Wild Billionaire
How to Tempt the Off-Limits Billionaire

Harlequin Desire

At the Rancher's Pleasure
Homecoming Heartbreaker
How to Handle a Heartbreaker

Visit the Author Profile page
at Harlequin.com for more titles.

PROLOGUE

Five years ago...

JAGO FOUND HER in her grandmother's bedroom upstairs, seated on the end of her bed, slim arms wrapped around a framed photograph of Lily, her red head bowed. She'd refused to wear funeral black and Jago thought that she looked even smaller in her simple ecru dress and low heels—if that were at all possible. Smaller, defenceless, broken.

He watched a tear drop from her nose onto the old wooden floorboards and swallowed, fighting the urge to turn around and rejoin the wake downstairs. What was he doing here? Sure, he'd known her for years and, through Thadie, interacted with her at Le Roux family functions, but they weren't *friends*. The best he could call them was friendly acquaintances. But he'd had his eyes on her all afternoon and when she ran up the stairs, obviously needing a break from her grandmother's mourners, he found himself following her.

Jago pushed his hand through his hair and rubbed his jaw, unable to take his eyes off her bright, bowed head, her pale profile. Love—that messy, uncontrollable, bewildering emotion—and its sidekick, grief, annihilated people. Like a lightning strike, it was powerful and destructive, diving towards its destination, fast and unforgiving, incinerating anything and everyone in its path. It was merciless, thoughtless, devastating.

Was it any wonder he avoided it?

Jago laid a broad hand on Dodi's head, and she looked up at him, her nose red from weeping and those marvellous grey-blue eyes drenched with tears. Despite the gravity of the occasion, her eyes held all the impact of a pole slamming into his stomach. He wished he could describe the colour accurately, but he wasn't a writer or a poet and the best he could come up with was that the smoky blue reminded him of sun-and-rain-splattered mist.

The first time he'd noticed her, six or so years ago, he'd been walking into a restaurant, his new bride, Anju, on his arm. He immediately noticed the redhead laughing with his sister, dressed in a short, boldly patterned sundress. Pretty, he'd decided. Young, and if she was a friend of his sister's, probably a little rebellious. Then someone had congratulated him, and Dodi was forgotten.

Too many deaths had occurred between that low-key celebration of his marriage to Anju and today: too many tears had been shed, too many floors paced and too many nights spent awake and grieving.

Jago gently pulled the photograph from her grip and placed it on the dressing table behind him. Having buried his wife and father months apart, Jago knew what Dodi was going through and what her immediate future held. After their funerals, he'd spent so much time dissecting his intellectual marriage, based on friendship and mutual interests, and examining his relationship with his volatile father. He knew that Dodi, in the weeks and months to come, would also do some intense soul searching.

But, unlike him, Dodi would grieve solo, without the support of family or siblings. Thadie, lovely and loyal, was trying to fill in the gaps but she couldn't be there twenty-four-seven for Dodi.

His heart, withered as it was, ached for her.

Jago sat down on the bed next to her, sliding his hand up and down her back, his hand connecting with every bump in her spine. She was so slight, so petite. Still, at only twenty-four, so damn young. 'How are you doing, Elodie Kate?'

He felt, rather than heard, her emotional hiccup to his using her full name. He had decided, years ago, that her old-fashioned name suited her ethereal face and slim build. And, as far as he knew, he was the only person who called her by her birth name. Jago knew it frustrated her but that wasn't a good enough reason for him not to use it. He liked her full name, so he'd use it.

Obviously exhausted, Dodi simply rested her head on his shoulder. Death, he realised, tended to put inconsequential arguments into perspective.

'I feel like a part of my soul has been amputated. It's just such a damned waste, Jago. Lily wasn't that old.'

Jago silently agreed. He didn't know Dodi's grandmother well but, from what he'd heard from his sister

Thadie, he understood Lily to have been a vibrant and charismatic woman, energetic and charming. She'd taken Dodi in when she was a teenager and Dodi adored her, as did his sister. Lily's death would leave a huge hole in Thadie's life and a crater in Dodi's.

Dodi curled into his arm and lifted her hand to his chest. Despite the sombre moment, he couldn't help his immediate reaction to her touch, the electric current to his groin. What on earth…?

This was his sister's best friend, someone he'd come up here to comfort, not seduce. She was grieving, sadness rolled off her in waves, but all he could think about was whether her mouth was spicy or sweet and whether her skin was as silky soft as it looked.

Jago shook his head, annoyed with himself. What was he thinking? Not only was Dodi grieving but she was also nine years younger than him and his sister's best friend, and his wife had only been dead a year. His reaction to Dodi annoyed and upset him—he loathed feeling out of control. He was not his father, easily able to move on from grief and loss.

But holding Dodi like this was torture.

Jago ran a tired hand over his eyes and shifted away from Dodi, who promptly followed and cuddled closer as if seeking his warmth.

Dodi wiped her eyes with the heels of her hands. Jago managed a tiny smile. It was the same gesture his nephews used when they were upset or tired.

'She left me her business, but I don't think I can take it on, Jago,' she murmured.

Jago sighed, wrapped his arm around her shoulder

and tipped his head sideways so that his head touched hers. 'Why not?'

'Because it makes me feel trapped,' Dodi whispered. Before he could ask her to explain her strange comment, she spoke again. 'We did everything together. She was my anchor.'

What was he supposed to say to that? He was self-sufficient and unemotional, deliberately so, and he had no words of comfort.

Dodi hiccupped a sob. 'God, Jago, what am I going to do?' she wailed as tears rolled down her face and storms rumbled in her eyes.

He felt out of his depth, uncomfortable, but what did that matter when he'd do anything to alleviate the emotional storm sweeping through her? 'What can I do, Dodi? Tell me, sweetheart, how can I help you?'

Dodi lifted her incredible eyes, and they collided with his, sparked and held. Half turning to face him, she rested her forehead against his. 'Help me forget, Jago, if only for a little while. Please, just give me that.'

He was shocked when her lips brushed his, transferring lightning from her mouth to his. He tried to pull away, but she just followed, her hands stroking his chest, her tongue in his mouth. Suddenly it was too much, she was irresistible, and his arm banded around her and he tumbled into a world he didn't know existed.

She tasted of mint and madness, grief and sadness. He knew this was the wrong time and place, that she was feeling overwhelmed and out of control, but he needed to learn her taste, have her scent lodged in his nose, feel her slim body pressed up against his. Her bottom was fuller than he'd expected, her hips curvier, and her breast filled his hand perfectly.

Jago pulled her dress up her slim thigh, sighing when she shivered, feeling more like a man than he ever had before. And yes, her skin did feel like warm silk, her hair smelled like sunshine and underneath his hand her heart, like his, triple-thumped.

He, suddenly and powerfully, longed to see her naked. He needed to know her, to count every freckle, to stroke every curve. He craved the feel of her long legs around his waist. It was vital to experience her feminine heat, to lodge himself inside her.

Forgetting where they were, who he was, Jago pulled her down to the bed, his hand encircling her thigh, his mouth fused to hers. Time stopped and the world stopped turning and there was only Dodi…

But Thadie, calling Dodi's name, shattered the moment. Dodi reacted quicker than he did, bolting off the bed and running for the bedroom door. He was still trying to process why his arms were empty when Dodi stepped out of the bedroom to meet Thadie in the hallway, pulling the bedroom door shut behind her and keeping his presence a secret.

Jago sat on the end of the bed for a long, long time, his head in his hands, mentally whipping himself for his lack of self-control. Then he left the bedroom and walked out of her house and out of her life.

Dodi had made him lose control. That was unacceptable and so she must be avoided.

CHAPTER ONE

DODI DAVIS STOOD just inside the front door of Love & Enchantment, the bridal shop she had inherited from her grandmother, Lily, and tried to ignore the familiar burn somewhere around her heart.

Wasn't it the law somewhere that the owner of a shop providing wedding dresses and accessories to excited brides be...well, excited?

Or, at the very least, believe in marriage and love and happy-ever-afters?

Dodi didn't.

'Dan didn't work out, but when you find the right man you'll feel differently, darling,' Lily had said, sounding completely convinced days before she died five years ago. Dodi hadn't wanted to argue with the woman who'd been her port in every storm, the one adult in her life who'd given her love and attention, who'd made her feel safe. A few weeks after her devastating diagnosis, they'd discussed her dying—her doctors had suggested she had just three months, if that—and what came next. It had been a horrible, awful, wretched conversation. Tears streaming, she couldn't tell Lily that she'd seen the worst of love, that she didn't believe in it and certainly didn't want to spend her life promoting the scam.

Lily, ravaged by cancer, hadn't needed the reminder that her son and daughter-in-law's lives had been a roller coaster of never-ending drama.

Dodi's parents had separated when she was three, divorced when she was four. Remarried when she was twelve and divorced when she was fourteen. In between their marriages and affairs, her dad had married once and her mother twice. Dodi vaguely remembered her one stepmother and two stepfathers but had lost count of the number of partners and lovers she'd met along the way.

Her parents liked variety and lots of it. To her parents love was possession and passion, and she was collateral damage—a human pass-the-parcel—lost and forgotten in their quest to chase down their next sexual or emotional high.

About a month before Lily's death, Dodi had got a call that rocked her world, shattered her soul. The caller told her that she'd been having an affair with Dan—her first real friend, her first lover and the man she'd thought she'd be with for ever—and that she wasn't the first lover he'd had...*that year.*

Dodi had immediately launched into a 'stand by your man' and 'he wouldn't do that' series of protestations, but the caller had proof, photos and text messages, and credit card receipts for hotels and dinners for two at places she'd never visited.

Dan's lover, sick of playing second fiddle, had also gleefully informed her that he'd played a series of mind games with her since the day they met and that his proclamations of love and forever were a lie. She'd had to face the hard truth that her best friend, the person she trusted and loved, second only to Lily, had cheated on her, more than once and with more than one woman.

Emotionally numb, she'd delayed confronting Dan until after Lily's death, partly because she couldn't deal with another emotional fallout as she watched Lily die, and partly because she hadn't wanted to upset Lily, who'd adored Dan.

Lily had had a near-perfect marriage, cut short by her grandpa's heart attack, and she'd loved love, loved her store and loved her only grandchild. So, to Lily, it made sense for Dodi to inherit Love & Enchantment, her renowned bridal boutique situated in Melville, an arty and bohemian suburb of Johannesburg, South Africa's economic powerhouse.

She loved this city, built on gold and one of the biggest on the continent. She loved its vibrancy and its crazy drivers, its fast-paced hustle and its blend of communities and nationalities. She loved the vitality of Soweto, the messiness of Alex, the gentility of Rosebank. She adored its cold winter days and, when the wild storms pounded it during its hot summers, its unapologetic in-your-face energy.

Love & Enchantment contained the largest selection of sample wedding dresses and bridesmaid gowns in the country and showed off the skills, artistry and creativity of the most elite wedding dress designers in the world.

Dodi appreciated the product but wasn't a fan of what the dresses, and all the other accessories—

bridesmaid and flower girl dresses, veils, shoes and bling—represented. Standing in the empty salon, Dodi felt like a fraud, trapped and frustrated.

Just once, she wanted to *choose* the situation she found herself in…

She'd been bounced between her parents' homes, and when she was sixteen she'd been, without discussion or warning, dumped with her grandmother, someone she'd never met. Dan's cheating and gaslighting had devastated her and Love & Enchantment had been forced on her…

Okay, enough, stop! You sound like an ungrateful brat!

Her childhood was *over*, Dodi told herself, and Dan was a mistake she'd never repeat as she was done with relationships. Moving in with Lily was the *best* thing that had ever happened to her and how *dared* she complain about inheriting Lily's considerable assets and fantastic business? If she hated the shop so much, then why hadn't she sold it, moved away, done something different?

She'd studied design at university, then pursued an additional business degree, thinking she'd like to travel before joining an upmarket retailer as a trendspotter or a buyer for retail fashion. She'd travel the world, wear designer threads, liaise with the top designers in the world…

She was months off graduating when Lily had died, and she'd inherited Love & Enchantment. Her two degrees enabled her to run the business without making too many mistakes that might have been hard to come back from, and provided her with a healthy income. Her house was paid for, as was this building.

But she still felt resentful of having her choices ripped away from her.

Get over yourself!

L&E was her link to the one person who had loved her unconditionally, who'd been her port after a lifetime of storms, her true north… Her loyalty to Lily was absolute. In life and death.

Dodi raised a bottle of water to her lips, sipped and eyed the big clock on the far wall. She had a half-hour before her after-hours, top-secret appointment. All her staff, except for her most experienced fitter, had left the premises and she was going to deal with the next bride, and her entourage, all on her own.

Dodi smiled, thinking of the uptick in appointments at L&E since Thadie Le Roux, body-positive influencer, socialite and heiress, had announced on Instagram that she was acquiring both her wedding gowns—one for the church, one for the reception—through Love & Enchantment.

Everyone wanted to follow in Thadie's footsteps and Dodi didn't blame them—her best friend was not only beautiful but also funny, down-to-earth and genuinely lovely.

And she was getting married at the end of May, tying herself to a famous and revered rugby-player-turned-sports-commentator. Clyde, having taken his young, inexperienced team to a World Cup Rugby win, was a national treasure and universally adored. Dodi rested her water bottle against her forehead, wishing she could warm to Thadie's fiancé.

Clyde had never been anything but charming to her, his future wife's closest friend. He was always thoughtful, considerate, respectful, but something about him bugged her.

Dodi bit her bottom lip and rocked on her heels. Did she automatically distrust every man she met because of her parents' dysfunctional relationships and because of what Dan had done to her? Was she projecting her fears about relationships and marriage onto Thadie?

She didn't know. Maybe. Possibly.

Dodi looked through the floor-to-ceiling windows and noticed the tall figure of Jago Le Roux crossing the road, looking ever so fine in his custom-made Italian suit, as well as crisp and cool despite its being a warm summer evening in Johannesburg. She immediately thought of her favourite broody heroes—Heathcliff from *Wuthering Heights* and Oliver Mellors, Lady Chatterley's gamekeeper. Like them, Jago was a corralled tornado of darkness and intensity.

Every time she saw Jago she was immediately whisked back to Lily's wake, remembering their passion-filled kiss, the strength of his arms as he had held her to his very fit body. For days, and weeks, before and after Lily's death, she'd felt as though she was encased in a cold, wet bubble, the real world distorted and distant. Jago's kiss had pierced her balloon of grief and loneliness and for five minutes—ten?—she'd felt alive, feminine, strong. Free of grief.

If Thadie hadn't interrupted them, God knew how far they would've gone. Pretty far, she reluctantly admitted.

God, he was good-looking. Tall, broad, fit, debonair, suave, her best friend's older brother turned heads, produced swoon-worthy sighs, and caused cars to crash into lamp posts. Dodi desperately wished she was immune to his sex appeal.

But, from the first time she'd seen him, and every time since, tingles raced along her skin, and fireworks exploded deep inside whenever she laid eyes on him. Yeah, she was attracted to Jago Le Roux—any woman with a pulse would be. But, she reminded herself, it was inherited lust, something left over from Neanderthal Dodi, whose survival had rested on mating with the most alpha of alpha men.

It was biology. It didn't mean anything. One of the lessons she had learned from living with her lust-soaked parents and cheating ex was that desire was ephemeral, as tangible as the early-morning mist hovering at the beginning of a hot summer's day. It could alleviate boredom, scratch an itch, be entertainment or, like their hot encounter after Lily's funeral, be a means of distraction and comfort. It didn't mean anything and never lasted.

Dodi flipped open the lock on her door and pulled it open to allow Jago to step through. She caught the delicious scent of his cologne and noticed his broad hand as he pushed his long fingers into his light brown hair, short at the sides, wavy on top, sun-kissed. The late-afternoon sun turned his three-day stubble to a deep gold.

It was early evening, but the dipping African sun sent bright yellow rays, tinged with pink, through her extensive showroom, dropping a flushed hue onto the bridal gowns hanging off copper pipe railings encircling the room. With its exposed wooden beams and skylights, the room looked huge, with clusters of vintage designer furniture in front of many floor-to-ceiling mirrors. Flowers, roses, sweet-peas and peonies gently scented her luxurious boutique.

Jago, so masculine, should have looked out of place in the faded peaches, creams and pinks of the bridal salon but, annoyingly, didn't. If anything, the super-feminine room just highlighted his masculinity.

'Dodi.'

'Jago.'

Their eyes collided and held, his gaze mesmerising. His eye colour ranged from pewter to steel to iron, occasionally shot with lightning, frequently rumbling with thunder. Hypnotic and spellbinding.

Despite being friends with his sister since they were in their late teens, she'd had little to do with the older of Thadie's brothers. Micah, his minutes-younger twin, was the more charming of the two. Jago was the string pulled too tight, about to snap. He was aloof, abrupt, introverted and broody, and those silver eyes, the irises surrounded by a black ring, were too scalpel-sharp for comfort.

He made her feel off centre, squidgy, jittery, and his effect on her irritated Dodi. She was almost thirty and should be able to admit that she was sexually attracted to the man and then move the hell on. But no, just looking at him made her feel like she was riding an out-of-control roller coaster.

Sanguine she was not.

'I'm glad I caught you alone,' Jago said, his deep baritone sending a shiver up and down her spine. He had the ultimate bedroom voice, rich and dark, like the Belgian chocolate she so adored. Great, now she was thinking about him in a bedroom, about pushing that jacket off his shoulders, pulling his shirt from the band of his trousers, laying her hands on his hot skin.

Argh! Seriously, what is wrong with you, woman?

Dodi folded her arms against her chest, conscious of her messy hair—it always was by the end of the day—and that the minimal make-up she wore had probably disappeared hours ago. She pushed the front door closed, locking it, and turned to walk into her salon, her right ankle slightly twisting and causing her to stumble. Jago reached for her and stopped her from falling flat on her face. Dodi found herself up close and personal with him, and God, he smelled so good. Of rich soap and laundry detergent, of a citrusy cologne and male skin. She wanted to bury her nose in his neck and commit his scent to memory. And Lord, every inch she touched was hard muscle and the hand that held her hip, steadying her, was big and broad and seared her skin.

Dodi looked up, and up, saw that his eyes were on her mouth and sparks skittered up and down her spine. She wondered whether he still tasted as deep and dark as she remembered, his kisses as rich as velvet, as smooth as heavy silk. For a moment, just a couple of seconds, she saw temptation in his eyes, desire deepening the silver to slate-grey, and in a flash his expression turned impassive, his eyes shuttered.

Right, the moment had passed but Dodi suspected her fair skin remained fire-red, almost the same colour as her hair. She remembered his earlier comment about being alone. 'Um...right...why did you need to see me alone?'

Jago took a moment to answer her. Was he also feeling caught off guard? No, not possible. Jago Le Roux, Johannesburg's toughest deal-maker, was always in control.

He hadn't been in control in Lily's bedroom... Stop it, Dodi!

'I wanted to catch you before the others arrived because I need to pay for Thadie's wedding dresses,' Jago told her, reaching into the inner pocket of his jacket to pull out a slim wallet.

Right. Of course!

Dodi nodded, remembering Thadie's offhand comment that her mega-successful brothers would be paying for her dresses, the bridesmaids dresses and all the wedding expenses. Her brothers had accompanied Thadie months ago to help her choose her dress, both feeling out of their depth and trying to hide it. It was a testament to the siblings' close relationship that they were back for this final fitting.

They were there as a stand-in for their dad, who had passed away five years ago. That had been a terrible year for both her and the Le Rouxs with Anju, Jago's wife, dying in January, Theo, the Le Roux patriarch, in March, and Lily six months later. They'd all attended far too many funerals that year.

But even before Anju died, and possibly due to the nine-year age difference between them, Dodi hadn't had much to do with Jago and had seen little of him. Thadie had had nothing in common with Jago's highly intellectual, aloof wife and tended to avoid her. Because Thadie and Anju weren't close, Dodi had only seen Anju a few times a year when she was invited to a function at Hadleigh House and, beyond saying hello, they didn't engage.

'Can I pay by credit card?' Jago asked her, pulling her attention back to their conversation.

'Absolutely,' Dodi replied, relieved. She'd paid the designer for Thadie's dresses earlier this week and had winced at her low bank balance after the transaction. She'd emailed both Micah and Jago, gently requesting payment, and here Jago was, thank God. Wedding dresses for high-society influencers were not cheap and she'd prayed one of the brothers would offer up his credit card this evening.

Someone upstairs had been listening.

'My office manager isn't here but I have a card machine in my office,' Dodi said. She thought about asking him to follow her and quickly discarded that idea. Her office looked like a bomb had hit it. Books of sample fabrics were stacked high, client folders needing to be filed were stacked even higher and her desk was covered with papers and coffee cups. It looked nothing like her exquisitely decorated showroom. 'Let me get it and the invoice.'

Luckily Thadie's file was on the top of the stack, and she'd printed the invoice out earlier. She grabbed the credit card machine, returned to the main salon and sat down at one of the many sofas in the room, all grouped around daises and oversized mirrors. She gestured for Jago to take the seat beside her and waited as he shed his jacket and slowly rolled up the sleeves of his cotton shirt, revealing tanned, muscular forearms lightly dusted with bronze hair. He had great hands, broad and strong. His fingers were long, with neatly clipped, clean nails. She had a thing about hands…

Dodi sighed. *Face it, Davis, you have a thing about Jago.*

Jago sat, pulled the knot of his tie down and flicked open the button holding his collar closed. Tearing her gaze away from his tanned throat, Dodi flipped open the file and picked up the invoice. She mentally grimaced at the total and handed it over.

There had been no discussion about what the wedding gowns would cost—Thadie had ordered two, one for the church and one for the reception—and, despite their wealth, she had no doubt the total would be a shock.

Jago looked down at the invoice in his hand and his eyes widened. 'I think you've made a mistake, Dodi.'

She shook her head, keeping her face impassive. 'I really haven't. And that's the discounted price as I gave you my friends and family rate.' Because Thadie was her best friend and she'd garnered an enormous amount of publicity having her as her client, she'd only added a small mark-up onto the cost, just enough to cover the expenses of shipping the dresses from Milan to Johannesburg.

'Forty-two thousand *US* dollars? Twenty for one and twenty-two for another?'

Was his deep voice suddenly an octave higher or was she just imagining it? Dodi nodded. 'They are Paulo Du Pont creations, Jago. He's one of the best wedding dress designers in the world. If not *the* best.'

'Holy crap. I could buy a very decent car with that sort of money,' Jago said, sounding a little strangled.

Dodi leaned back and crossed her legs, not worried. Jago, along with Micah, having inherited the extensive multinational company his father built from a small corner grocery store he established when he was twenty, was an exceptionally wealthy man. The Le Roux twins owned mines and manufacturing plants, shopping malls and farms, hotels and chain stores, both in Africa and overseas.

Dodi found running one business strenuous enough. She had no idea how the brothers kept track of multiple businesses, thousands of employees, managers and billions in assets. But their long hours working were paying off because Le Roux International was still expanding and was, thanks to Jago's and Micah's hard work as co-CEOs, stunningly successful.

As shareholders, Jago, Micah, Thadie and Liyana—Theo's second wife and Thadie's mum—topped the richest people in the country list. Dodi was pretty well off—she'd inherited all of Elodie's wealth, a house in a gated community in the wealthy area of Blair Atholl, northeast of the city centre, and this building—but the Le Rouxs operated in another stratosphere.

Dodi knew Jago's credit card could handle a forty-two-thousand-dollar charge. Hell, she was pretty sure it could handle any amount thrown at it. With certain cards, unlimited meant exactly that and she was pretty sure Jago owned one or two, or ten, of those types of credit cards. And a mega-healthy bank balance to support his purchases.

Dodi heard Jago's sigh and watched as he pulled a

card from his wallet and handed it over. It was sleek, black and heavier than any other bank card she'd ever handled. She recognised the familiar logo but not its weight. 'Why is it heavy?' she asked as she swiped the card through the machine.

Jago shrugged. 'It's made from titanium.'

Even her machine was impressed by the card because it pushed through Jago's transaction at double its normal speed. Dodi pulled off the receipt and handed the card and paper back to Jago, her fingers brushing his. Sparks danced along her skin as desire flared in his eyes and she fought the urge to kiss his sexy mouth.

Nobody, before, or since, had kissed her the way he had. With casual confidence, incredible skill and soul-deep passion.

Jago's eyes dropped to her lips and all the moisture disappeared from her mouth. 'Do you ever think about the kiss we shared back then?' he asked, his thumb caressing her index finger, which was still holding his card. How could such a small amount of skin on skin cause such havoc?

Of course she thought about it! Every day. Sometimes more than once. But she couldn't tell him that. 'Do you?' she countered on a whisper, still unable to pull her hand away.

'Yes.'

How often? When? What do you remember? It took all her willpower to keep her questions behind her teeth. And even more not to dive in for a repeat performance. It had been so long since she'd been kissed by anyone, let alone someone with superior skill.

Jago tugged his card from her grip and Dodi blinked, then blushed. She sat back and pushed her hand through her hair, telling herself to stop acting like a complete dolt! It was a quick kiss, nothing special…

If she'd been kissed more, had more people kiss her, she wouldn't think about him so often. It was simply a question of numbers…

Right.

Dodi needed to put some distance between them, some time to gather her thoughts. Dodi folded the invoice in two, handed it to Jago and tapped the credit card machine with her finger. 'I'm just going to put the machine and Thadie's folder away, so that she doesn't see either when she arrives.'

Jago nodded. 'Good idea. If she sees what the dresses cost, she'll insist on paying for them herself, and that's not going to happen. Her wedding is our gift to her and Clyde.'

Dodi saw doubt flicker in Jago's eyes at the mention of his soon-to-be brother-in-law and tipped her head to the side. Did Jago not like Clyde or was her imagination running wild? She dismissed her suspicions, thinking she was doing Clyde a disservice. As she well knew, breaking into the Le Roux inner circle was incredibly hard and Thadie's brothers were intimidating. They were both tough, take-no-prisoners direct. They were successful, supremely wealthy, incredibly powerful men and Thadie wasn't a shrinking violet either.

She'd known the family for a decade and when she attended the odd function at Hadleigh House, the Le

Roux family home, she still felt like an outsider looking in. Clyde needed time to fit in.

'Paying for her wedding is an incredibly generous gift,' Dodi commented.

Jago shrugged. 'It's what my father would've done. He wouldn't have spared any expense, and neither will we.'

Dodi kept her eyes on his tanned face, taking in the finer details of his masculine features. He was in his late thirties—thirty-eight to be precise—and long hours working had put tiny lines next to his eyes, grooves next to his mouth. He was a stunningly good-looking man, but even hot guys couldn't stop life from leaving its marks on their faces.

And why did she feel the urge to smooth his frown, to kiss his tension away? To wrap her arms around his very broad back and hug away his stress? And then take him to bed to make him forget?

Wow! Where had all that come from?

They'd been talking about Thadie's wedding and her out-of-control imagination—or her libido—had steered her in a completely different direction.

Enough of that, Davis!

They'd had a moment years ago, for God's sake! Jago Le Roux was her best friend's brother and completely out of bounds. And way, *way* out of her league.

Walk away, dump your stuff and find your brain, Dodi.

CHAPTER TWO

DODI WALKED AWAY and Jago tipped his wrist to look at his watch and wished he were back in his penthouse office suite, working. He felt out of place in this peach and pink feminine room, and a huge sneeze, brought on by the subtle scent of what had to be dozens of cut flowers, threatened. Pushing it back, he rested his forearms on his knees, and swiped his thumb across the screen of his smartphone. Within the emails he saw one with the subject name 'Lagos' and his thumb hovered over it, poised to open it. He knew the email pertained to a shopping mall they were building in the city and scrolled down. The real estate, retail and hospitality arms of the business were Micah's baby and he had enough on his plate dealing with the mining, manufacturing and agricultural businesses in their portfolio. Jago watched as new messages and emails landed, feeling incredibly weary. Needing a break, he pushed the side button and his screen turned black. He placed his phone on the cushion next to him and rubbed the back of his neck. Work never stopped and he took calls and received emails and texts twenty-four-seven.

He and Micah could both do with a clone, or three. And that was why he didn't have the time or energy to waste looking at wedding dresses in ultra-pretty salons. He wouldn't be here for anyone else but Thadie. He—and Micah—would move mountains stone by stone for their baby sister.

Jago watched as Dodi crossed the room to a wedding-dress-lined hallway. This was only the second time he'd been in her shop—or any bridal salon. Anju, the least interested bride in history, had worn a cream trouser suit to their civil wedding and hadn't bothered with a bouquet. Afterwards, they had both gone back to work and met up with his family later for dinner at a local restaurant.

They'd spent nothing on their wedding, but Thadie's wedding was edging close to a million. If not a lot more. Dodi's wedding dresses cost the price of a small car. *Each.* The champagne was imported, as was the caviar. The caterers were the best in the country and the entertainment was a hot Los Angeles singer-songwriter he'd never heard of.

It was pure insanity. Jago rubbed his jaw and reminded himself that his dad would've paid anything to give Thadie what she wanted. And more. There was no doubt that Thadie had been his favourite child, the apple of his eye, the one who could do no wrong. And, in this instance, he agreed with his father. Thadie, along with her twin boys, was—and always would be—the best part of their lives.

Jago looked at Dodi's slim back, his eyes trailing over the loose curls of her long hair as she stopped in the hallway and straightened a picture frame. Over the years her bold red hair had deepened to a deep Titian red and yeah, with her willowy build, pale skin and flowing locks, she looked like a muse of those pre-Raphaelite artists. She was missing the melancholic expression though, as her feelings raced across her face and jumped into her smoky blue eyes.

And yes, she had freckles—how could she not with her complexion? Lots and lots of them, darker on her straight, haughty nose, paler across her cheeks and forehead.

After losing his self-control after Lily's funeral, Jago had deliberately avoided Dodi. When he had to be in her company, he ignored her as much as possible, acting as if their kiss hadn't redefined the word for him. Before that sad day, the connection of lips had been another GPS point on the route to the destination—a great orgasm. It was enjoyable, sure, but not, to his mind, necessary. Everything had changed when he kissed Dodi. He'd never admit this, not even under extreme torture, but as his mouth had met hers he felt the DNA that formed the stars and the starfish, the mammoths and man, luminesce deep inside him. When he had kissed her, touched her fabulous skin, he felt for the first time in months and years alive and connected.

And utterly out of control.

He still thanked God Thadie had chosen that moment to call Dodi, to break their passionate connection. She'd saved him when he hadn't been able to save himself…

But, damn it, his attraction to her hadn't faded, not even a little. When he'd caught Dodi after her stumble earlier, his body immediately sat up and started taking notes. Sexy mouth, great breasts, long legs he wanted to feel wrapped around his hips. She smelled of soap and lemongrass, of blue skies and fresh air, and the combination of her slim body, her scent and those witchy eyes stopped him in his tracks. And sent his blood rushing south.

Jago rubbed his hand over his face. What was it about her that turned him inside out? Could it be because he hadn't had sex for a while? Damn, he hoped so! Maybe he should schedule a visit to one of a handful of old friends who knew the score, a woman happy enough to share his bed and who wouldn't sulk when he left it a few hours later. Sex had always been—yeah, even with Anju—a physical release, a way to blow off steam. As necessary as exercise and sleep.

The fact that he'd reacted to Dodi—his sister's best friend!—was a solid clue that he needed to get some. And soon.

Jago looked around the expensive salon and curled his lip at the wedding dresses on rails encircling the three walls of the room. There were hundreds more in the back, simple and stylish, splendid and luxurious. Shapes and cuts and decorations to suit every taste, ranging from mildly expensive to eye-wateringly and budget-blowingly insane. He could not understand why women put so much stock in looking like a hyped-up, photoshopped version of themselves, why they put so much time and effort and money into one night, the adult equivalent of their first school dance.

Why they even wanted to get married in the first place.

Having been there, done the whole thing, he knew

of what he spoke. Would he marry again? No. Not because he'd been unhappy in his marriage—he hadn't been particularly happy either, truth be told—but because marriage was an outdated institution that had little relevance in today's world. He'd been twenty-seven when they married. They made their relationship legal because Anju, despite being a brilliant neuroscientist with a glittering future ahead of her, craved financial security, a legal document, and a solid prenup agreement.

Because she was what he'd wanted, an unemotional woman who didn't demand love, loved sex, good food and travelling, he agreed to her terms. Fiercely intelligent, she wasn't interested in having kids, and apart from having enough money for a roof over her head and food in the fridge, didn't care that he was the son of a multibillionaire. She also had an equally low tolerance for drama. They'd loved each other, he supposed, and he'd grieved for her when she died. But life went on and here he was, five years after her death, still single, and still allergic to drama.

He'd had so much of it as a kid, before and after his mum died when he was nine. They said that his father was larger than life, charismatic and compelling, brilliant, but, to Jago, he'd been intensely volatile, a bully and a bastard. For his entire early childhood Jago stood on the lip of a volcano, constantly scanning the horizon for trouble, for a hard wind or quick tap that would push him—or his mum and brother—into the lava that was Theo's temper. They never knew where they stood with him, and their home swung from laughter to tears in the space of a heartbeat. His father could slow dance his mum around the kitchen one second and throw a crystal glass against the wall the next.

Jago did everything he could to keep the peace and, before his tenth birthday, became adept at scanning his environment, looking for problems and trying to head off trouble. But, as hard as he tried, he couldn't anticipate that his mum would die in a head-on collision or that Theo would start dating six weeks after her funeral. His marriage to Liyana, four months after his mom's death, rocked him. And once Liyana moved into their home, it was as if his mum had never existed. Theo, his dad, refused to talk about her and redecorated their home top to bottom, expunging everything she'd done to make their house a home. Theo donated everything of hers—from jewellery to art to clothes to trinkets—to charity. He tossed out all the family photographs, effectively erasing her presence in their life as a surgeon would cut out a cancerous tumour.

Before Jago had hit puberty, he decided that love equalled drama and he wanted nothing to do with either concept.

Jago heard a brisk knock on the front door and looked around to see his twin, Micah, and Thadie standing under the rounded peach portico above Dodi's front door. Seeing no sign of Dodi, he stood up and walked across the salon, twisting the key and pulling open her door. Thadie stepped into the salon, followed by one of her bridesmaids—Alta, Clyde's stepsister, agent and publicist. Having only met her once before, he stuck out his hand and internally sighed when Alta kissed his right cheek and then his left. He caught Micah's eye and frowned at his twin's knowing smirk.

Micah knew better than to think he had the hots for the very spiky Alta: she was too in-your-face and too abrasive for him to make a move in her direction. He had no idea why his laid-back sister had included her in the wedding party. It had to be a request from Clyde. Nothing else made sense. And Alta, he was sure, had only agreed to be a bridesmaid to stay in the wedding loop and to make sure nothing tainted or tarnished Clyde's glittering reputation.

Thadie pulled him into a hard hug. She had her famous mother's cut-glass cheekbones, warm brown skin, face and height but Jago still saw her as a wide-eyed kid with knobbly knees. In his head, she definitively wasn't old enough to be a mum or to get married.

He adored her.

Thadie stepped back from him and looked around the salon, before releasing a long sigh. 'I love this place, and I still expect Granny Lily to walk in from the back with a huge smile on her face.'

His sister had the biggest heart in the world. 'You really liked her, didn't you?'

Thadie sent him a soft smile. 'I did. She was truly lovely. Dodi is a lot like her.' Thadie looked past him, and her smile rushed into her eyes. 'Hey, you!'

Jago knew, without turning, that she was talking to Dodi, as they were always excited to see each other.

Jago moved and saw Dodi standing there and his heart rate, stupid thing, accelerated. She'd tidied her hair and reapplied her lipstick and her right arm was fully extended over her head. Two clothing bags brushed the floor. Jago quickly moved towards her and took the bags from her, his height making it easy to hold them off the floor.

Dodi thanked him, greeted Micah and Alta and smiled at Thadie, who was hopping from foot to foot in excitement. 'Are those my dresses?' Thadie demanded.

Dodi mock frowned at her. 'Your dresses? What dresses? Did you order a dress from me?'

Thadie rolled her eyes at Dodi's teasing and reached for the zip of one of the bags. 'Lemme see.'

Dodi gently smacked her hand away. 'Be patient, Thads.' Dodi gestured to a whitewashed credenza standing against the far wall. On it stood a silver ice bucket containing a bottle of champagne and champagne flutes. 'Have a glass, then join me in the first dressing room on the right and let's see what they look like.'

'I hope they are perfect,' Alta commented. She tapped the face of her watch with a red-tipped fingernail. 'You're running out of time, and you'll be in a world of hurt if they don't fit.'

Jago watched, fascinated, as Dodi's eyes cooled, and her expression flattened. 'We're not in the habit of making mistakes, Alta.'

Alta lifted her too-thin eyebrows. 'I hope not because, as you know, this is the wedding of the year.'

Jago watched the storm brewing in Dodi's eyes and waited for her sharp comeback. But instead of issuing a harsh retort, she pulled up a smile and took Thadie's hand. 'Lily would haunt me if we messed up your dresses, Thads, you know that.'

Her gaze moved from Thadie to the front door and

Jago saw the rest of the bridal party, his stepmother Liyana and Thadie's two other bridesmaids, approaching the salon.

'Micah, if you could open the front door for me, that would be wonderful and then give the ladies a glass of champagne, please. I'm going to help Thadie change into her gowns, and then we'll choose the mother of the bride and the bridesmaid dresses. Sound good?'

No, Jago silently replied. It sounded like hell, actually.

Dodi didn't wait for their agreement, she just led Thadie out of the room, their hands linked. Dodi's melodious voice drifted back to him as he followed them to a changing room with the wedding dresses. 'We might have to make some very minor adjustments, Thads, just to make sure the gowns fit beautifully. But, because they are Paulo Du Pont gowns, I'm not expecting any problems.'

At twenty thousand US dollars a dress, Jago bloody well hoped not.

Dodi closed the door behind Thadie, Micah, Liyana and Thadie's other bridesmaids, flipping the lock and her sign to *CLOSED* to keep out any late evening shoppers or spur-of-the-moment drop-ins.

Kicking off her heels, Dodi moved over to the seating area and jerked when she noticed Jago standing by the window that looked out onto the small garden to the side of the property. She'd had her hands full with Thadie's mum—the very discerning ex-supermodel Liyana—and the ultra-picky Alta, who had something negative to say about every bridesmaid dress she suggested. Micah excused himself after seeing Thadie's dresses and she'd thought that Jago left too, so she was very surprised to see him in her now empty salon…

Surprised and excited. Seriously? Excited by Jago Le Roux? Was she losing it? Yes, he was stunningly sexy, but she'd sworn off men, and relationships. Because, really, she never knew what to expect from people in general and men in particular.

'You're still here,' Dodi commented as he picked up a champagne glass.

'I thought I'd help you clean up.'

Since Jago Le Roux had been raised with a full set of silver cutlery in his mouth, his offer came as a surprise. The Le Roux family employed a butler and a houseful of servants. Had the man ever made a bed, washed dishes? She didn't think so.

'Where do you want them?' he asked.

Dodi looked at the delicate glasses he held and thought that with one small squeeze from those big hands they would shatter. 'Uh… I'll get a tray from the break room.'

He picked up the other glasses. 'No point, I'll just carry them through. Where to?'

Dodi gave him directions—down the hallway, last room on the right—and he was back within a minute, his face bemused. 'I feel like I've been sucked into an alternative world of silk and satin. How many wedding dresses do you have in stock?'

She wrinkled her nose. 'Including the stock that came in today, probably close to three hundred.'

His eyes widened. 'Seriously?'

'Some, depending on the designer, are hugely popular, some aren't. Some, not many, thank God, don't have any takers at all. We auction those online to raise money for women's shelters and organisations dealing in domestic violence.'

He sat down on the ottoman she had used earlier. 'Do you pick the dresses yourself or do the designers just send you a range of their designs?'

Dodi was bemused by his interest. She'd never imagined that Jago Le Roux would be interested in her shop and that he would engage her in a getting-to-know-you conversation. She didn't know what to make of it. 'A mixture of both. I sit down with my head of Sales, and we choose what we like and what we don't, taking into account what's hot and what's not. We then order sample dresses of the designs we like. We also allow the designers to send us a few dresses they think we should stock. The brides try on the sample dresses, and if they want that particular style we measure them and put in an order for the dress. Six to eight months later, the dresses arrive, and we pray the bride hasn't lost or put on too much weight.'

'Thadie's wasn't predesigned, was it?'

She smiled. 'No, Thadie's was specifically designed for her.'

He jammed his hands into the pockets of his trousers and rocked on his heels. 'Can you explain how a dress can cost so much damn money?'

She heard the puzzled note in his voice, the confusion. And yeah, she got it, it was an insane amount of money to spend on a dress, but she'd had brides who'd spent more. Not many, admittedly. 'Real pearls and Swarovski crystals, high-grade silk, handcrafted embroidery, French Chantilly lace and fabric. Shall I go on?'

'No, you are giving me a headache.'

She smiled at his low rumble, knowing that it wasn't the money he was complaining about, because Jago wouldn't deny his sister anything. He, like most men, simply didn't understand that beauty and craftsmanship also applied to clothing and not just to things with engines.

Thadie's dresses were works of art, completely stunning. They were some of Paulo's best work. And, because they were incredible and for a VVIP client, she'd lock the dresses in the walk-in safe in her office before she left for home. Her staff had all signed non-disclosure agreements, but anyone could take a sneak peek of the gown and snap a photo on their phone. She had over thirty consultants and knew that most had offers from tabloid reporters to spill the beans on their high-value clients.

Not on her watch.

Dodi perched on the arm of a wingback chair, swinging her bare foot. She really should slip on her heels, but this was Jago, the shop was closed, and she didn't think he cared. He took a long moment to answer, and she was fascinated by the emotion in his normally unreadable eyes. 'She's going to make the most beautiful bride,' he stated. Thadie was lovely, inside and out, but it was nice to hear Jago state the obvious.

'She really is,' Dodi agreed.

'And you handled Alta well,' he told her, surprising her. 'She was demanding and annoying, but you didn't lose your cool.'

Dodi shrugged, then smiled. 'I've had a lot of practice at not losing my cool. Trust me, she wasn't the most difficult client I've had this month. Or even this week.'

Jago winced. 'I would've lost patience five minutes in,' he admitted. She didn't doubt it. In the business world, Jago wasn't someone to be messed with. He had a reputation for being cold, unfeeling, decisive and determined. It was commonly accepted that, with Jago, you had two choices: either move out of his way or get run over.

'Good job, Elodie Kate.' Elodie Kate? Her grandmother was the only person who had ever called her by her full name—Dodi was a nickname everyone used—and she swallowed, emotion closing her throat. Man, she still missed Lily with every beat of her heart. She should be here, running this shop, bestowing her wide smile and good sense on neurotic brides, scared brides, spoiled brides. She could charm bridezillas into behaving better, shy brides into happy conversations and tame off-the-wall brides.

Unlike Dodi, she hadn't pulled on a mask and gritted her teeth as brides gushed and giggled, cried and cooed.

Really, what the hell had Lily been thinking, leaving her L&E?

And why did Jago's compliments make her feel warm and wonderful? They had a tenuous connection because of her friendship with his sister, and shared a brief kiss years ago, nothing more. They were, essentially, little more than strangers.

Maybe it was because he was so difficult to impress. He set, as she'd heard from Thadie, impossibly high standards for his employees.

And himself.

Jago looked at the expensive watch on his wrist and grimaced. 'I should go. I still have a lot to do tonight.'

She looked up to find his eyes on her face and she sucked in a sharp breath, unable to look away. Those eyes! Intense and piercing and so very, very captivating. He had the eyes of a warlock, she decided. And his face and body weren't too bad either.

Not bad? He was utterly gorgeous! Why did her skin feel too tight for her body? Why did she suddenly want his lips on hers, his hands on her back, her breasts, her bum? What was happening here?

His gaze travelled up and down her body, and flames licked her skin. Her feet were glued to the floor and the room felt smaller. And a hundred degrees hotter. Dodi heard Jago release a small expletive, and within a second, maybe two, he crossed the space to where she sat, slid his hands under her elbows and lifted her to her feet. His big hand slid around to her back, and he held her against him, but Dodi knew that with a small push he'd release her and step away.

Honestly? She rather liked where she was, thank you very much. His chest was broad, hard muscles covered by hot skin and fine Egyptian cotton. He smelled like summer, of thunderstorms and hard rain, lemons and deep forests.

She lifted her hand to touch his jaw, trailing her fingers through his surprisingly soft stubble, enjoying the feel of his hard, square jaw. Her thumb brushed over his bottom lip, and she heard his low growl again, the one that made her feel squidgy and soft, superfeminine.

This was crazy, this was wrong…this was Jago! But she couldn't, wouldn't, step away, not until she'd reacquainted herself with how he tasted, until she'd discovered whether there was still passion behind his inscrutable, abrupt facade.

Despite being tall, Dodi still had to lift onto her toes for her mouth to reach his. Please, please don't rebuff me, she silently begged. Give me this one kiss, this one moment out of time.

She tasted his sigh, sweet and a little desperate, and when his lips didn't move to meet hers she thought, for one awful moment, that she'd miscalculated, that he didn't want to kiss her.

But she caught the smallest twist of his lips, a flash of lightning in his eyes, and his mouth covered hers, a petrol bomb tossed into a dry wooden shack. Flames, hot and insistent, scampered across her body, and her nerve endings caught fire. Dodi slid her hand under the collar of his shirt to find warm male skin and curled his fingers around his strong neck. She sighed, and when Jago's tongue painted the seam of her mouth with need and fire she opened her lips and…

Boom! Electricity shot to her toes, up her legs, into her womb. She wanted to protest, rail at him for making her feel so out of control—no one had ever made her feel so alive!—and at the same time she wanted to climb inside him, be part of him. His arms tightened around her, and his big hand slid down, cupping her butt and pulling her closer so that her stomach pushed into his heavy, hard erection, as he easily held her against his hard, muscular frame.

This was heaven, she decided, and hell. Heaven because his kiss was more powerful than the one they'd shared before. Hell because she knew they had to stop before they went too far. She couldn't make love to her best friend's brother on her shop floor on a Wednesday evening in late summer.

She couldn't make love to her best friend's brother at all!

This was an aberration, a crazy, tiny rip in reality. And this didn't mean anything, it couldn't. She wouldn't let it.

But surely she could keep kissing him, just for a little while longer?

His stubble tickled as he dragged his lips to her cheekbone, teased her jawbone. Keeping one hand on her butt cheek, he moved the other between them and found her breast. The material of her dress and bra was an unwelcome barrier as he massaged her nipple and teased it into a hard peak. She felt her panties dampen and when his hand rucked her dress up her thigh and his fingers encircled the top of her leg she knew they had to stop because if he kissed her one more time, if he touched her there, she would be lost…

And she didn't know if she'd be able to find her way home.

Dodi, reluctantly, it had to be said, pushed her hands against his chest. 'Jago, stop.'

It took a couple more kisses and his fingers skimming the front of her panties before her words registered.

He pulled back and glowered at her, disappointment in his eyes and rushing across his face. 'We're stopping?'

'Yes.'

He dropped a harsh curse into the heavy silence that followed her answer. *'Why?'*

Dodi stepped back and shook out her skirt. 'Because I'm not making love in front of floor-to-ceiling windows, because you're Thadie's brother, because, despite that connection, you're just one step up from being a stranger!'

'I've known you since you were eighteen years old! We've even kissed before!'

'That kiss didn't count!' Dodi retorted. 'I was sad and hurting and you were trying to comfort me, to make me feel better. And in the ten years we've known each other,' Dodi added in a rush of words, 'we've never had a conversation that went beyond *Hi, how are you?* I don't know what madness this is but it's stopping right now. I'm not interested in a relationship—'

'It was a kiss, not an invitation for you to move into my life!' Jago responded, his eyes reverting to their normal sub-zero silver.

She ground her back teeth together, quite sure enamel was flying from her teeth. 'I don't do one-night stands, Le Roux, and I know that's all you do.'

'Have you been following my love life, Elodie Kate?'

Oh, he was now starting to annoy her. But, unlike when she was with her picky brides, she didn't have to keep her sharp tongue behind her teeth. 'In your dreams, Jago. I don't care who you sleep with, as long as it's not me.'

'Your kiss two minutes ago tells me that statement is a lie. This time, you're not sad or in need of a distraction. Are you?'

She winced and felt herself flush. She *so* wasn't going to answer that question! Their conversation was getting out of control, and she needed to shut it down. Pronto.

Dodi lifted her nose, spun on her heel and walked over to the front door, flipping the lock to open. She yanked the door wide and gestured for him to leave. 'Let's pretend this never happened, Jago,' she said, injecting a healthy amount of frost into her words.

He took his time walking towards her, reminding Dodi of a stalking cat, leashed power about to erupt. He reached her, looked down at her and then, surprisingly, his mouth twitched in amusement. He dropped his head to speak in her ear. 'This is far from over, sweetheart.'

CHAPTER THREE

JAGO THREW HIMSELF into his brand-new Range Rover Autobiography and scowled at the passing traffic. He pulled his hand down his face, rubbing the palm of his hand along his jaw. What the hell was that?

Stupid question, Le Roux.

That was lust. Flat out, intense desire. Drop-her-to-the-floor-and-take-her-now attraction.

For the past five years, he'd made a conscious effort not to think about Dodi and their kiss, to ignore her as much as possible. But their collision just now—what else could he call it?—blasted through his carefully constructed shields. Thoughts he'd pushed away came rushing back in with the force of a nuclear-powered rocket...

He adored her thick, dark red hair that made him think of Ireland and mystics and magic. Her voice held a hint of gravel, a rasp that deepened when she was turned on, and her eyes were a lovely, strange shade of smoky blue. Or were they wispy grey? Her young, too-thin frame had slid into curves, and her legs went on for ever, legs he wanted to explore with his hands, then his mouth and his tongue.

Jago leaned back in his seat and gripped the steering wheel, his knuckles white against the black leather. Annoyingly, he could still taste Dodi on his tongue, almost feel those full, soft lips against his, her nipple spiking the palm of his hand. Today's kiss had nothing to do with grief, wasn't a way to ease her sadness. No, what happened earlier was pure, clean desire…

And deeply dangerous.

She was his sister's friend, someone who'd hovered on the outskirts for years, but here she was, front and centre, in his life. Jago tightened his grip on the steering wheel, holding on so that he didn't fling himself out of his car, run across the road and finish what they had started. Oh, he'd never force her—he wasn't, and would never be, that guy—but he knew that a few hot kisses would melt their clothes away.

He wanted that more than he wanted to take his next breath.

He didn't like feeling so out of control, being at the mercy of his emotions and desires. He operated best when he had mental and emotional guardrails in place, and to keep them erect and functioning meant keeping control.

Kissing Dodi—Dodi herself—blew a series of holes through those barriers. And that was utterly unacceptable. Control was everything.

He'd seen how destructive it was living with a mercurial and volatile personality, so when he'd met Anju he'd known she was exactly what he wanted, what he needed. Someone cool, detached, someone who abhorred drama. From their first date, he'd known their life together would be calm, smooth sailing, unaffected by high emotion. He'd liked her very masculine way of looking at life, that she was always rational.

They hadn't needed to have intense, soulful conversations—Anju was very like his father in that regard. Theo hadn't been one to interrogate feelings, to acknowledge hurts, to admit anything in his perfect, perfect world was wrong. His father had the incredible ability to compartmentalise his life, and if a person or a set of circumstances didn't fit into his worldview he was quickly able to move it into his not-important-enough-to-waste-energy-on box. Anju had been the same, adept at moving on. But, because their relationship was based on mutual respect, equal intelligence, shared priorities, he didn't feel the need to be constantly on the lookout, waiting and watching with anxiety, and they made their marriage work. Theirs had been a meeting of minds…

Unlike his encounter with Dodi. He felt unhinged, out of control, as if he'd been plugged into an electrical socket. Jago pushed his thumbs and index fingers into his eye sockets, hoping to push away his sudden headache.

Dodi was unexpected, their kiss unanticipated, his world a little shaken.

Jago had no problem admitting he felt uncomfortable with change, with the unforeseen, was easily rattled when situations didn't play out as expected. He'd spent his childhood and teenage years trying to anticipate trouble, trying to prepare for a change in his mercurial father's mood. Overanalysing everything in an attempt to avoid emotional meltdowns from his father. That was why Anju had been perfect for him. She was constantly calm, effortlessly undramatic. She'd been a respite from a stormy life spent with his father.

The hoot of a car horn, then the shouts of a taxi driver half falling out of his window in an attempt to attract some customers, jerked Jago back to the present. How had he gone from thinking about his volcano-hot encounter with Dodi to thinking of his past, his father and his wife? He must be more stressed than he thought. Tired too.

But if being around Dodi triggered these reminiscences then maybe it was better if he avoided her from now on. They'd had little to do with each other since they met. Surely they could carry on that fine tradition?

Except that he and Micah were part of the wedding party, Dodi was Thadie's maid of honour and they'd have to be in each other's company more than usual in the build-up to the wedding. Thadie's engagement party, delayed because of Clyde's work commitments, was this coming Saturday, then there were the hen and stag parties, both of which he'd have to attend.

He'd rather shove a lump of burning coal in his eye.

But his non-appearance would hurt Thadie, and he refused to do that. He'd do anything and everything for his siblings.

And if that meant feeling like he was dancing on the edge of a razor-sharp blade or connected to a thousand volts of electricity whenever he came within a few feet of Elodie Kate, then he'd just have to deal with it.

He was a big boy. He could handle it. And her.

* * *

'I thought redheads weren't supposed to wear red. Or pink.'

Dodi turned at the deep, rich voice in her ear, cursing the goosebumps pebbling her skin. A few words, two short sentences and she wanted to melt into a puddle at his feet. Utterly ridiculous. Could she be any more asinine if she tried? She was almost thirty and a hot guy in a designer suit shouldn't have this mind-melting effect on her.

Dodi touched the pleated skirt of her halter-neck, sleeveless cocktail dress, a bright, bold red ending with an eight-inch block of bright pink. It was, she admitted, a bold choice but Liyana, Thadie's mum, reassured her that the dress looked fabulous, and the colour suited her complexion. Since Liyana was fashion-obsessed and had exquisite taste, Dodi trusted her assessment.

'I seldom do what people expect,' Dodi told him, thinking how amazing he looked in his custom-made, perfectly fitting dark grey suit, striped shirt and a tie the colour of a rich, fat aubergine. A paisley handkerchief peeked out of the pocket above his heart. He had what Lily called a clotheshorse body: wide shoulders, slim hips, long legs. Honestly, Jago could make a priest's robes look sexy.

Her inner fashionista nodded in approval. 'Bold colour combination, Le Roux. I didn't think you had it in you.'

He touched the knot of his perfectly formed tie. 'Credit to my stylist. She puts these combinations together. I just take the complete outfit off the hanger and pull the clothes on.' He straightened his waistcoat before shrugging his shoulders. 'I don't care much about clothes.'

Sacrilege! 'I do. I love fabric and fashion, clothes, interior design. Anything that's design-led.'

Jago snagged two glasses of champagne from a passing waiter's tray and passed one to Dodi, who shivered when his fingers brushed hers. How old was she? Twenty nine or nineteen?

Sipping, Dodi looked across the entertainment deck of Jago's childhood home and into a garden filled with shadows, smiling at the fairy lights wound around the trunks and branches of the old oak trees. She wasn't a regular visitor to this house and the last time she'd been here was to attend Theo's post-funeral wake.

Hadleigh House was one of the great historic homes of Johannesburg, built in 1904 by one of the city's first mining magnates. She'd always loved this house, constructed in Arts and Crafts style with touches of the Art Nouveau movement. It was an enormous double-storey house with a shingled roof, and some windows still sported leaded light glass within their frames.

She remembered hearing that the first owners of the house were, like Jago's parents, incredible hosts and the Hadleigh House balls, tennis parties and Sunday luncheons were the stuff of legend. Most of the original grounds surrounding the house had been sold off but the extensive garden was still wonderful, with old oak trees standing sentinel over wide, thoughtfully planted wide beds. The entertainment area ran the long length of the house and flowed onto an enormous pool, and at the end of the garden stood a tennis court and pavilion. Tonight their guests, immaculately dressed, stood around the pool or sat on comfortable sofas and chairs, enjoying the warm, scented air, excellent canapes and the steady supply of expensive alcohol. Occasionally they wandered down paths leading to secret gardens and courtyards, complete with deep ponds housing fat, and happy, koi fish.

Dodi saw Thadie standing next to the dessert buffet laid out by the pool, Clyde's proprietary arm around her waist. They were talking to Liyana, a grey-haired man and a woman who had the look of a long-distance runner. Wait, wasn't that…?

'I didn't know Thadie was friends with the British ambassador and the country's favourite Olympian,' Dodi commented, tipping her glass in their direction.

'She isn't. But Liyana, with input from Clyde, drew up the guest list,' Jago replied. 'The opportunity to network must never be missed.'

He definitively sounded cynical. 'And you? Don't you need to network?' Dodi asked him.

'No,' Jago stated. 'People either want to do business with me or don't. I'm not the type to schmooze.'

'You really need to work on your confidence, Jago,' she sarcastically murmured.

He flashed that rare smile, the one that hit his eyes, and Dodi had to look away. That particular smile could be used as a weapon of mass destruction.

Right, moving on…

Dodi's eyes bounced off more guests and then she saw Micah talking to Alta, Clyde's stepsister dressed in a barely-there mini-dress. She grinned. 'Your brother doesn't seem to have the same problem.'

Jago's thick eyebrows pulled together. 'He'd better be careful because she is actively looking for husband number three.'

'What happened to numbers one and two?'

'Both marriages ended in divorce. Hopefully, the third time is the charm but she's wasting her time looking for a commitment from Micah.' Jago took her hand and led her to a quiet corner of the expansive entertainment area, pulling her behind two huge Ficus trees so that they were half hidden from curious eyes. He nodded to her dress. 'You do look amazing, Elodie Kate.'

He had once told her that her old-fashioned name suited her and, as he was the only person who called her by it since Lily, and both times in private, she didn't mind. Pleased by the compliment—such an ego boost coming from the super-sexy, normally reserved Jago—Dodi hoped the darkness hid her heightened colour. 'Thank you.'

They were silent for a few moments before Jago spoke again. 'You said you loved fashion, clothes…'

'I do,' she replied when his words trailed off.

'But not wedding dresses?'

Surprised by his prescience, she felt her champagne glass wobble in her hand. 'I don't know what you are talking about,' she stated, cursing the unsteady note she heard in her voice.

Although he stood in the shadows, she saw his small shrug. 'I think you do.'

Was he just shooting in the dark or was her antipathy towards Love & Enchantment not the closely held secret she thought it was? She'd never spoken to anyone about her feelings towards L&E, not even Thadie. Admitting that she hated weddings, and wedding dresses, made her feel disloyal to her grandmother, as if she was throwing Lily's hard work and sacrifices in her face.

Dodi sighed and stared out into the darkness. Nobody understood how difficult it was to be the object her parents fought over, not because they loved her but because they didn't. Neither had they wanted to be saddled with her. She'd learned some major life lessons before she hit double digits: that nothing was permanent, that relationships were only temporary and that getting attached was a good way to get hurt. She'd loathed her life, being bounced between her parents' houses, and frequently wished she lived anywhere else.

She got that wish when her father—Lily's only child—had left her at Lily's house without forewarning or an explanation. Up until that point, shortly before her sixteenth birthday, she hadn't known of Lily's existence. After a few weeks and being unable to contact either of her parents, Lily enrolled her in school, and she was given chores and rules and regulations.

She wanted to hate Lily and her new life, but she didn't, couldn't. Lily was lovely, kind but firm, and so very normal. Life with Lily was so much better, more stable than what she'd ever experienced before. But what she did hate was her lack of choice, the fact that her path had been chosen for her and that her future had been moulded by another's hand. Being bounced between her parents, coming to live with Lily, inheriting the business…none of those life-changing events was her choice.

After Dan's infidelity and Lily's death—the first a real betrayal, the second that felt like one—she vowed she'd never allow anyone to dictate the terms of her life again, to make decisions for her.

But Jago's sensing of her feelings towards her business was a red flag, an indication that he saw too deeply and too much. *So why did he think that?*

He shrugged at her question. 'When you get excited, your eyes turn a deeper shade of blue…some of the smoke clears.'

What was he talking about? 'My eyes change colour?'

'Mmm.'

'You're talking rubbish, Jago.'

Jago leaned his shoulder into the wall and crossed one ankle over the other. 'No, I don't think I'm off base at all. The other day your eyes were a flat grey. I think you appreciate the dresses for their workmanship and beauty but they don't touch your soul. Do you only feel like that about Thadie's dress or *all* wedding dresses?'

'I don't feel like that at all,' Dodi told him, irritated.

'Liar,' Jago softly responded. One corner of his mouth kicked up. 'And, since those dresses cost me a fortune, I'm bloody offended.'

He was nothing of the sort, he was just teasing her. And that was a surprise because she hadn't thought Jago Le Roux knew the meaning of the word. She knew him to be terse and abrupt, aloof and distant. She didn't know how to handle a teasing Jago and, because she also wanted to move the conversation along, she thought it prudent to change the subject.

An obvious choice was this house and its recently completed renovations.

'Why did you decide to renovate the house? It was pretty wonderful before.'

Jago narrowed his eyes, obviously debating whether to pursue his interrogation. Thankfully, he looked around and nodded. 'It had some structural issues. The roof needed replacing, some of the foundations were sinking. The house, originally, had eight bedrooms but some of the rooms were dark and gloomy so we created five suites, all with en-suite bathrooms. We also created two separate wings at the back of the house with two master bedrooms and two lounges, and separate entrances so that Micah and I can have some privacy when we want it.'

'And Liyana lives in the house behind this one.'

Jago nodded. 'When she's in the country, which isn't that often, to be honest. Our stepmama is a bit of a social butterfly.'

Since it wasn't unusual for Liyana to be photographed at an event in Monaco on Wednesday and in New York on Friday, that was the understatement of the year.

'We wanted Thadie to move in, but she said that living with Liyana, or us, would drive her mad. She compromised by buying her place just down the road.'

Yeah, there was a reason why this street in the ultra-wealthy suburb of Sandhurst was unofficially known as Le Roux Drive.

'What will you do if either you or Micah marry? Who gets the house?' Dodi asked, intrigued.

'Technically, as the older son, I inherited the house,' Jago replied. 'But this is Micah's childhood home too so we designed the renovations in such a way that we both, should that ever happen, could easily have two still ridiculously big but separate homes. We'd share the hall and the entertainment deck and, obviously, the pool and the grounds. And Jabu.'

They both turned to look at Hadleigh House's butler, a distinguished gentleman who'd been with the family since the twins were toddlers. Jabu, hands behind his back, was watching the hired catering staff with an eagle eye as well as waiting for orders from any members of the Le Roux clan.

He was, she knew, adored by everyone in the family and was, as Thadie informed her, constantly bombarded with offers of employment. Jago followed her gaze. 'He had two job offers this week,' Jago told her. 'One from a Japanese businessman who spends half a year in Joburg, another from the Bahraini ambassador's wife. One of these days he's going to leave us for a more exciting position.'

'What makes you say that?' Dodi asked him, touched and a little amused at his glum tone.

'He's made it very clear that we don't entertain enough, that there's not enough to do, that Micah and I work too hard, and that this house needs a young family. Or families.'

Yep, definitely morose. 'And do you plan on doing something about his demands?'

'I'm smarter than that,' Jago told her, his expression turning sly. 'His biggest complaint is that there are no small children around, so whenever he gets broody I send him around to Thadie's place and she lets him look after the twins for a day. He comes back shattered and doesn't nag us for a week or two.'

Dodi's laugh tumbled over her lips. She'd seen the normally staid and distinguished Jabu running after Thadie's Energizer Bunny three-year-old twin boys but hadn't realised how they exhausted the older man. Or the motivations behind why the brilliant butler was playing nanny.

'He desperately wants more Le Roux grandchildren, but he's equally terrified he might be saddled with more boys. After all, the man barely survived Micah and me.'

Dodi shook her head, still laughing. 'C'mon, you couldn't have been that bad!'

'We were his worst nightmare. Frogs and sugar in beds, sliding down the bannisters in the great hall, throwing darts at old paintings,' Jago told her, his affection for Jabu shining in his eyes. 'What else? Food colouring in the pool, dyeing our white Labrador green. Making chlorine bombs and trying to jump off the turret roof onto mattresses—'

Dodi grimaced. 'No way!'

'We were monsters. Occasionally, I remind him of how bad we were and that also shuts him up for a while,' Jago said, smiling. He really should smile more often, Dodi thought. Smiles belonged on that sexy face.

'Do you want a tour?' Jago asked, standing up straight. 'Would you like to see what we've done to the house?'

CHAPTER FOUR

DODI NODDED AND Jago plucked her glass from her hand, placed it on the nearest table and, taking her hand, led her around the corner of the house. It was darker here in the shadows and she tightened her grip on Jago's hand, trusting where he led.

He tested a handle, a door opened and Jago tugged her into another dark space. He told her it was their home gym and sauna. 'I'm not going to turn on the lights—I don't want to attract attention.'

He pulled her past a kick bag hanging from the ceiling, and as her eyes adjusted she noticed the different machines, all top of the line. Right, that explained his beautiful body under the excellent suit.

They emerged into a hallway and to the right, at the end of the passage, she saw a chic, extra-large kitchen—black granite surfaces and matte black ply doors and drawers—filled with the catering staff. Jago turned left and Dodi followed him, idly noting the incredible art on the walls. She passed a Tretchikoff, a massive Blessing Ngobeni, and an exceptional William Kentridge. The passage bent right and ended in a rather prosaic set of stairs, the exact opposite of the magnificent, hand-turned wooden staircase dominating the main hall of the residence.

'This was originally the servants' staircase. There's another one on the other side of the kitchen. We can, obviously, access our suites via the main hallway but this is a more private entrance.'

Dodi licked her lips as she followed him up the stairs onto a landing that overlooked the hallway that doubled as a fantastic space for entertaining. Keeping to the shadows, they looked down at the guests below, some of whom were listening to the four-man jazz band playing in the corner, some quietly talking in small groups. Dodi allowed her fingers to drift over the shoulder of a bronze sculpture of a Khoisan hunter, his eyes squinting against the sun. She'd forgotten that Theo Le Roux had been such an avid collector of art, sculpture and ceramics.

'Your house is amazing,' Dodi told Jago, still conscious that her hand was in his. She tried to tug it away, but he tightened his grip as he led her down the gallery and another hall, passing a series of closed doors.

He stopped at the end of the passage, pushed open an oversized door and stepped back to let her walk inside. The door clicked closed behind him and Jago tapped a screen on the wall next to the door and a soft, warm light filled the room. Dodi looked around, intrigued. Like the rest of the house, his sitting room was exquisitely decorated, with rich cream walls featuring amazing seascapes from artists at the top of their game. Two leather sofas and an oatmeal-coloured wingback chair faced a massive flat screen on the wall.

But, unlike the rest of the exquisitely decorated house, this room looked lived-in, loved. A haphazard pile of books sat on the coffee table, there was a dirty coffee cup on the side table and a sweatshirt lay across the back of the chair. A pair of top-of-the-range trainers sat on the ancient, massive Persian carpet. A sleek laptop lay on the cushion of one of the sofas.

Jago shrugged out of his jacket, pulled down his tie and opened the buttons to his waistcoat. 'Take a seat,' he told her, heading to the corner of the room, where two walls filled with bookshelves met. Pulling a bottle of red wine from the built-in wine rack, he held it up. 'Would you like a glass?'

Dodi narrowed her eyes at the expensive label. 'I'm not a wine connoisseur, so maybe you shouldn't waste your good wine on a plebeian like me.'

Jago gave her another half-smile, efficiently removed the cork and poured wine into two huge glasses. He walked over to her, handing her the glass before sinking into the depths of his enormous sofa. She could imagine him falling asleep there, weary after a long workday.

Dodi, still standing, sipped her wine—fruity and rich and, yes, delicious—and sauntered over to the bookcases to inspect his reading material. Books on politics were mixed in with crime thrillers, autobiographies stood alongside business tomes. 'How on earth do you find a book?'

'I have a photographic memory,' Jago replied, crossing his feet at the ankles. 'I know where everything is, mostly.'

Dodi walked across the carpet to the open doors,

which led to a small patio. Peeking outside, she saw a wrought-iron table and a lovely, plump sofa squatting on the balcony—good grief, what was a Fendi Casa sofa doing on a balcony? It was a perfect place to drink an early morning coffee. She could hear the distant sounds of the party but, because they were on the other side of the house, the noise was a gentle wash in the background.

'Aren't your guests going to miss you?'

Jago shrugged. 'Micah did a "welcome to the family" speech on our behalf—he's better at that sort of stuff—and Liyana is playing hostess, backed up by my twin. And they know I hate crowds and won't be surprised by my disappearing act.'

She looked down at her feet. 'I can go if you want to be alone.' She forced herself to smile. 'But you might have to draw me a map so that I can find my way back to my car.'

Jago's eyes slammed into hers. 'I wouldn't have brought you up here, to my *private* living space, if I didn't want you here, Elodie Kate.'

Right. Well, then.

'Why don't you take a seat, kick off your shoes?' Jago suggested. He looked at her spiky heels and pulled a face. 'Those heels are super-sexy and do amazing things for your butt and legs, but they have to be as uncomfortable as all hell.'

She started to protest, saw the amusement in his eyes and shrugged. 'You're right, they are uncomfortable. But also very gorgeous.'

'That they are,' Jago agreed when Dodi sat down on the edge of the sofa and bent down to unbuckle the strap around her ankle. She murmured her relief and slipped off the other shoe, rotating her feet at the ankles.

'Pretty, pretty little instruments of torture,' Dodi murmured.

'Is there any point in asking why you wear them if they hurt? Or is that one of those inexplicable things women do that we will never understand?'

'As you said, butts and legs.' Dodi grinned, picked up her wine and pulled her feet under her bottom, her dress flowing over her knees and down her legs. Jago slid further down the sofa and rested his head against the back, looking relaxed for the first time that evening. Dodi tamped down the urge to run her fingers down his jaw, to rub her nose in the stubble on his cheeks.

By being here with him, feeling so comfortable in his space, she was playing with fire. If he kissed her, there was a very good chance of their clothes flying off. She wasn't sure if the idea excited or terrified her. Or both.

She nodded to a door on the other side of the room. 'Your bedroom?'

'Walk-in closet, bedroom and then a bathroom,' Jago replied. 'Feel free to take a look.'

Curious about him, and his space, she stood and walked into his bedroom, taking in the textured, deep navy walls and the enormous bed covered in white linen. Yet another wall was covered in shelves, the verdigris copper pipes and wooden shelves adding warmth to the room. A trio of atmospheric charcoal sketches in matt black frames caught her attention.

They were, she quickly realised, abstract portraits of Jago and his siblings.

This was another room that was lived-in. A jacket lay across the arm of a navy-and-grey-striped armchair. A book was face down on the side table. A huge window led onto yet another private balcony that looked over the back garden.

'Like it?'

Dodi felt his breath skimming across the top of her head, the words warming her from the inside out. She turned and found herself just an inch from him. One tiny step and she'd be in his arms, one lift of her toes and her mouth would reach his. Like before, the urge to kiss him was overwhelming, the need to be in his arms, her mouth under his, urgent.

He muttered a low, indistinguishable curse and placed his hands on her hips, gently pulling her towards him. She wanted to be sensible, to step away, but her body had other plans and she all but fell into his arms in her eagerness to get closer to him.

He looked down at her mouth before dragging his eyes up to slam into hers. 'I've told myself, over and over, that this is crazy, I have no idea where this need for you comes from but I'm tired of talking myself out of having you,' Jago murmured. 'I think I should and *must* kiss you…everywhere. Tell me you want me to do that.'

'I shouldn't but I do,' Dodi told him, reluctance tinging her words.

'Thank God.'

Jago nibbled her jaw, and she inhaled his cologne, and her mind went fuzzy. She lifted her chin to give him better access to the spot where her neck met her jaw, and he dropped an open-mouthed kiss on her skin.

Dodi released a turned-on groan. 'I want you, but I don't think this is a good idea, Jago.'

'Best idea I've had for a long time. Stop thinking, Elodie Kate, just feel.'

This wasn't her. She didn't find herself in the bedrooms of sexy billionaires who smelled of midnight and looked like temptation. She knew she should walk away, find her way through his enormous house and back to her car, but being sensible wasn't what she wanted to be tonight. She wanted to be a little wild, throw caution to the wind, step away from the reality of her life—working too hard and playing too little—and *feel*. She wanted to feel like a woman again, sexy, desired, wanted.

But…

Jago placed a hand on her heart, and her nipple under his hand reacted immediately, instinctively. 'Your eyes are blue fire and your heart is pounding. You want me, Dodi, as I want you.'

'I don't want to want you,' Dodi replied, sounding cross.

He smiled, amusement flashing in his eyes. 'Don't deny yourself—don't deny this, us. And, for God's sake, stop thinking. Give me one night, and we'll go back to normal tomorrow…whatever normal is.'

His words reassured Dodi a fraction, and she knew that Jago always kept his word. They could have their moment out of time and then it would be done, a nice memory, something to remember when she was old and grey. He wouldn't hassle her for another round, demand more, allude to it in conversation. Jago might not talk a lot, or hardly at all, but she trusted every word out of his mouth.

In the morning, when she was back at her house, this night would be a secret the two of them shared.

Dodi tapped her fingers to her mouth, knowing that she was on the slippery slope to saying yes, to sharing her body and this experience with a man who'd been on the periphery of her life for the last decade. She wasn't someone who indulged in casual encounters, who had one-night stands—this would be her first—but it had been so long since she'd been held, since she'd had her body stroked, since she'd heard a masculine voice in her ear telling her she was beautiful, how good she felt…

So long since she'd experienced the tangle of limbs, the rough texture of a man's skin, being rocketed up and up and feeling as if she could touch the stars.

She was a strong, independent, modern-day woman but even a strong woman needed to feel, if only for a few hours, sexy and desired, to lie within a strong man's arms.

'Come to bed with me, Elodie Kate,' Jago said, taking her hand and pulling her to the end of his massive bed. She expected him to kiss her, to follow up his suggestion with a sexy swipe of his lips, his tongue twisting around hers, but he pulled her against him, cuddling her to his chest, allowing her the space and time to make up her mind, to get her jumbled thoughts into some sort of order. Dodi slid her hands up and down his ribcage, feeling his hard muscles under the thin cotton of his shirt. She rested her nose in the vee of his open shirt and inhaled his scent—soap and cologne and a deeper note that was pure Jago. She touched her tongue to his skin and felt him shudder, relieved to know that she could make this terse, uncommunicative man tremble.

Emboldened, she pulled his shirt out from the band of his suit trousers and slid her hand under the fabric, allowing her fingers to skate over his ridged abdomen, his ribcage, through a light smattering of hair and over his flat nipples. She felt his tension, knew he was holding his breath, and when he spoke his voice was growly with frustration.

'Are we doing this or not, Dodi?'

Oh, yeah, they were. She couldn't *not*. She looked up at him through her long lashes and started to undo the remainder of his shirt buttons, pushing aside his shirt and vest to lie her hot mouth against his skin.

Jago placed his hand against her cheek, his thumb gently lifting her chin so that she had to look into his eyes. 'I need you to *tell* me that I can take you to bed, Elodie Kate.'

She nodded, but his eyes told her that her gesture wasn't good enough, so she licked her lips and forced the words over her dry tongue. 'Yes, Jago, just for tonight.'

'Thank God,' Jago muttered. He stepped closer to her, his fingers dipping down and lifting the hem of her dress to her thighs, and slid his thigh between her legs, creating a little friction, a lot of heat. Passion clouded his eyes as her hands skated over his wide chest. He brushed his thumb against her lip, over the throbbing pulse point in her throat, across one erect nipple.

So good, so amazingly wonderful.

Dodi didn't know that she'd spoken aloud until he responded. 'You are the sexiest thing I've ever seen. I can feel your heat on my leg, and I bet that if I put my hand between your legs I'll find you wet.'

Dodi released a breathy whimper.

His hand on her lower back pulled her against him and his erection jumped against the fabric of his suit trousers. 'Let me see you. I need to see if my imagination matches up to reality.'

His hands found the side zip to her dress, and he slowly, tantalisingly pulled it down, allowing the warm summer air to touch her skin. He unhooked the catch at the top of the zip and lifted the halter-neck over her head, exposing her pale cream braless chest to his heated gaze. She wanted to cover up but the admiration in his eyes gave her courage. He smiled as he skimmed his finger over her freckle-covered chest. 'You are more beautiful than I thought. And I love every dot,' he murmured, curling his hand around one of her breasts, always smaller than she'd like. He bent his head, sucked her nipple inside his mouth and Dodi whimpered with pleasure, sliding her fingers into his hair to hold him there.

Her dress whispered away, and Dodi found herself lying against the cool fabric of his duvet, with Jago exploring her body with his tongue and lips and those large, gentle hands.

She could lie here for ever, a goddess being worshipped, feeling languid and loved.

Jago pulled away from her to kick off his shoes, to discard his shirt and vest. She half sat, resting on her elbows as he revealed his big, beautiful body, fascinated by his arms bulging with muscle, the raised veins under the skin, his long, powerful legs. Broad hands and feet, and his fallen-angel face.

He was every inch a man and she felt feminine and powerful, a combination of goddess and muse.

Jago joined her on the bed and leaned over her, his mouth an inch from her own.

'One night, Elodie Kate, and let's make it one to remember.'

'One night, Jago. Kiss me…please.'

His eyes slammed into hers and she pushed her head back into the pillow, stunned by the blistering heat in his gaze. He wanted her. She was astonished by how much. Was there anything as wonderful as being the object of a hot, sexy guy's complete attention? She didn't think so.

Dodi ran her hands down his chest, her fingers flirting with the snap on his trousers. Jago looked down at her hands and smiled. 'Feel free to explore.'

'I would, but you haven't kissed me yet,' Dodi murmured.

He didn't need to be told twice, and as his skilled tongue slid into her mouth she—somehow—managed to push his trousers and his underwear down his hips, exposing gorgeous masculine skin she couldn't wait to explore. The dip of his spine, his long muscles flowing over his hips, his firm and masculine butt. After he removed the last of his clothing, Dodi lifted her hand to touch his face. She stroked her thumb over his jaw, along his cheekbone, explored the shell of his ear, dragged the tips of her fingers through the scruff on his face. If she only got to do this once—whose stupid idea was that?—she wanted to be able to pull up this memory. In years to come, she wanted to remember how he smelled, the heat of his skin, the rich taste of his mouth.

Dodi sighed as Jago's hands moved up and down her back, over her butt, up her sides, and onto her breasts. His touch was confident and assured. He was a man who knew how to touch a woman and make her burn.

Jago's fingers speared into her hair and he gripped the back of her head, taking their kiss deeper. With her entire focus on him and what he was doing to her, Dodi felt her control slipping away, superseded by the need for her to know him, in the most intimate way a woman could know a man. She tilted her hips up, needing to connect with his erection, to feel his need. For her.

So much need.

Jago moaned, a deep, guttural grunt of approval, and Dodi felt her panties slide down her hips, and, with no hesitation, he parted her legs and dragged his fingers across her feminine folds. Dodi whimpered and then gasped when his finger pushed inside her, his thumb on her tiny, responsive bundle of nerves.

'Condom,' Jago panted, pulling back to reach over her to open a bedside drawer. He pulled out a packet, ripped it open with an impatient curse and rolled it down his shaft. Resting his hands on either side of her head, he stared down at her, his eyes the colour of molten silver. 'You are exquisite, Elodie Kate.'

Emboldened by his compliment, Dodi streaked her hands over his upper body, trying to touch him wherever she could. She was burning up, a rocket flying through the atmosphere, and she needed him to push her through to the other side. 'Jago, I need you. Inside me. Now!'

He didn't argue, didn't hesitate, just entered her with one long, sure, perfect stroke. Dodi's legs encircled his hips and she pushed her nails into his firm butt, groaning with approval as he kissed her mouth, his tongue winding around hers.

He didn't move, but Dodi could feel his arms shaking, felt the tension in his neck, his back. Dodi jerked her hips up, trying to find her release, and softly cursed when Jago pulled back, keeping her hovering on the edge. Ducking his head, he pushed her breasts up so her nipples could meet his mouth.

Pleasure peaked and peaked again. She was so close. All she could think about, concentrate on, was the sizzle, waiting for the moment she burst into flames.

As if sensing she couldn't take any more, Jago drove into her, deeper and harder, demanding more from her. Her lungs tightened—who needed to breathe anyway?—her skin flushed, and her channel throbbed as she teetered on the edge of an earth-shattering climax.

He did something, she knew not what, and then her orgasm hit, incinerating her. But, strangely, she still needed more and she begged Jago not to stop. Knowing her body better than she did, he pushed his hand between them to find her nub while his hips pistoned into her. Dodi felt herself reignite, and when she felt his release she stepped into another fire, this one filled with pyrotechnics. She became colour, luminescence flowed through her veins, kaleidoscope patterns formed on her skin. Magic, witchery, sorcery…

She'd thought of him as a warlock and, man, maybe that description was closer to the truth than she'd realised.

CHAPTER FIVE

A LITTLE MORE than a month later, Jago looked up at the sharp rap on his door, looked through the glass—all the walls to their offices were glass—and gestured for Micah to come inside. He held up his index finger, asking Micah to wait, and returned his attention to the high-pitched squawking in his ear.

His head of Human Resources had a dozen reasons why her weekly report wasn't in his inbox and none of them held any water. Jago ended the call and shook his head. 'People,' he told Micah, knowing he'd understand his frustration.

'People,' Micah agreed.

Jago looked across the room to where Micah stood by the window, taking in the view of the sprawling city of Johannesburg from his admittedly impressive office. Both he and Micah negotiated with some of the most powerful men and women on the continent—politicians, dignitaries, and deal-makers—so when they'd had their offices redecorated a year ago they had wanted to impress. They'd demanded clean and streamlined decor, offices with the most up-to-date technologies, including touchless computing and big screens for remote conferencing. His space was elegant, luxurious but, because it was where he spent so much time, also comfortable. He liked it.

It was coming up for noon and the midsummer heat rising off the buildings made the dusty, smoggy air shimmer. Micah looked harassed, Jago realised, an unusual state for his normally sanguine twin. His hands were in the pockets of the grey designer chinos he'd teamed with a light blue shirt and a navy jacket. Because he had a meeting with conservative investors later, Jago wore another expensive suit—a navy blue stripe with a white shirt and burgundy tie. Boring as hell, he admitted. Dodi would not approve, but he looked sober and serious, exactly the impression he wanted to convey.

'What's up?' Jago asked Micah, forcing a memory of Dodi, lying naked on his bed, her red hair rippling across his pillow, freckles flowing across her satiny skin, away. It had been four, nearly five weeks since she'd left his house as the rising sun shattered the night, got into her car and driven away. Thirty-three days of silence, seven hundred and ninety-odd hours of trying not to think about her.

Of wanting her again, wishing he could have a replay of that truly spectacular night…

He saw Micah's mouth moving, realised he hadn't taken in anything and held up his hand. 'Sorry, say that again?'

Micah frowned at him. 'It's not like you to ask me to repeat myself…'

'It's been a long morning.'

Micah walked towards his desk and gripped the

back of one of his leather and chrome visitors' chairs, a deep frown pulling his eyebrows together. 'Thadie called me, in an absolute state. Someone cancelled their booking at the wedding venue.'

He didn't understand. 'What do you mean?'

'Somebody called up the venue, said she was Thadie's wedding planner—she actually used the wedding planner's name—and explained that the wedding was off and that they should keep the deposit for the inconvenience. The venue, as you know, has a waiting list a mile long and they've already slotted someone else in.'

It took Jago a few seconds to understand what he was hearing. 'Jesus...are you being serious?'

'Deadly.'

'But surely they'd check? The wedding is one of the biggest in the country—why would they dismiss such a huge event on a phone call?'

'Ah, it was followed up by an official-looking letter from the wedding planner and a fake email from Thadie.' Micah looked as if he was grinding his teeth. 'Could they have tried harder to confirm? Sure. But they had the deposit and another function to fill the space, so they weren't too concerned.'

What fresh hell was this? Jago rubbed the back of his neck as his brain kicked into gear. 'What now?'

'Well, apart from tracking down the person who sabotaged her big day—'

'Who would do that? And why?' Jago demanded.

'She's had an uptick of trolling on her social media accounts since their engagement was announced. There's been a raft of nasty comments but nothing that grabbed her attention. Unfortunately, she did name the venue on her social media feeds, so the world knew where they were going to hold the reception. Anybody could've cancelled it.

'We could sue, kick up a fuss, but it doesn't change the fact that we need to find a venue that can accommodate a thousand people in less than six weeks,' Micah pointed out. 'Thadie asked me for help. Thank God we own an events company so I'm roping in one of their top consultants to help me find a venue.'

'Great idea,' Jago replied. He looked away from Micah and through the glass walls of his office saw a flash of red hair topping a pale face. His heart pounding, he watched Dodi cross the large reception room, stopping to talk to his PA.

What the hell was she doing here? They had an agreement...*one* night. Then nothing. No contact.

And why did he feel so damn glad to see her? Why was his heart skidding around his ribcage?

Micah turned to see what had caught his attention. 'Dodi looks like she's in a strop,' he said. 'Thadie must've told her about losing the venue.'

That didn't explain why she was at Le Roux International, and not with their sister.

Dodi turned to look at him through the glass panes and their eyes clashed and held, hers turbulent. She looked paler than normal and had dark stripes under her eyes. He stood up, pushing his chair back so hard that it crashed against the credenza. He skirted his desk and yanked open his office door.

'Let her in,' he told his assistant.

'Your investors will be here in five minutes, Mr Le Roux.'

'I know,' he replied, his eyes not leaving Dodi's face. Yep, she looked as if she'd been handed a bag of Cape cobras or a pipe bomb. 'Come, Elodie Kate.'

The last time he'd said those two words aloud had been when he'd been painting her skin with his words and his kisses. She'd exploded on his mouth seconds later.

Not helpful, Le Roux.

Dodi nodded briefly and walked into his office, stopping in front of Micah to plant a kiss on one cheek, then another. He didn't get as much as a 'hello, Jago', never mind a kiss.

'I presume you are here to talk about the venue disaster,' Micah said, gesturing for her to take one of the two Wegner swivel chairs.

Dodi frowned, looked from Micah to him and back again. 'I'm sorry…what are you talking about?'

'Someone, a very cruel, malicious someone, cancelled the wedding venue and now Thadie and Clyde have nowhere to hold their wedding reception,' Micah explained.

'What?' Dodi's eyes widened and her freckles stood out against her white skin. She raised her fingers to her mouth, genuinely horrified.

'Didn't Thadie tell you?' Jago asked, puzzled. Didn't they share everything?

Dodi pulled a face. 'Uh…my phone has been off.' She bit her bottom lip. 'What are we going to do? How are we going to find another venue?'

Okay, it was obvious that she had no idea of the cancellation, so that begged the question…why was she here, in his building, demanding to see him? He thought they had an agreement that they'd only see each other when they both had to attend wedding-related events.

It was bad enough having her invade his thoughts and dreams at inopportune moments—or all the damn time—but seeing her in the flesh just made him want to strip her of that black sheath dress and wedge shoes, pull out the pins securing her messy hair to her head and lower her to his office sofa.

Again, not helping yourself, Le Roux.

'I'm on it,' Micah told her. 'I'm going to make some calls and get some help from another event planner.'

'I can ask some of my wedding contacts whether they have any ideas for a venue, if that will help,' Dodi suggested.

Micah nodded. 'Good idea, thanks.'

'But who would do this?' Dodi demanded, turning her clear gaze back to him. '*Why* would they do this? Thadie is the sweetest, nicest person around. She doesn't have enemies!'

It was a good question. Someone disliked his sister enough to cause her a lot of stress and anxiety and to spoil what was supposed to be the wedding of the year. Who? And why? And how the hell did they unmask someone working in the shadows?

They were burning questions, good questions, but another question was also burning a hole in his soul.

'If you didn't come here to discuss Thadie's wedding dramas, why are you here, Elodie Kate?' Jago asked as he resumed his seat behind his streamlined, modern desk, also a Hans Wegner design, linking his fingers across his stomach.

Every drop of colour disappeared from her face and anguish dropped into her smoky blue eyes. Jago, reading her body language, abruptly sat up and frowned. 'What is it, Dodi?'

Dodi looked at Micah and bit down on her bottom lip. 'Micah, would you mind giving us a minute?'

Micah's expression turned stubborn, a look Jago knew well. 'If this has anything to do with Thadie, then I have a right to know.'

Dodi shook her head, the fingers gripping the arm of her chair turning white. 'I promise you, it doesn't. I just need a private word with Jago and then I'll be on my way.'

Micah shot her a disbelieving look, but he did, thank God, walk to the door and yank it open. He shut it behind him and Dodi closed her eyes. Her lips moved silently, and Jago felt his heart sink to his toes.

Whatever she was about to say was going to change his life for ever. Of that he was sure.

Dodi lurched out of her seat and stomped over to the floor-to-ceiling window of his incredibly luxurious office, resting her throbbing head on the cool glass, oblivious to the amazing view of Johannesburg from the massive tinted windows. After a few days of feeling bone-deep tired, headachey and frustrated by a constant horrible metallic taste in her mouth, she'd decided a visit to her doctor might be in order. Since Dr Kate was one of her grandmother's oldest and best friends, her father's godmother and the woman she was named after, she could kill two birds with one stone: see her old friend and also get a Vitamin B injection to lift her energy levels.

But because Kate was the type of doctor who insisted on thoroughly checking her over she was there for the best part of an hour instead of a quick in-and-out visit. She'd also given her an astounding piece of news and Dodi, not thinking, had immediately turned her car around and headed into the city to Le Roux International's headquarters.

She now regretted that impulsive move. She wasn't ready to share her life-changing news with Jago. Oh, she'd have to, at some point, but she needed time to wrap her head around it first.

She needed to think, to assess, to make sense of it all.

She was pregnant, with Jago's baby.

She understood the individual words, but the sentence still didn't make sense. How had this happened? Why? Why her? Why with him? Dodi wanted to release the pressure pressing against her ribs, to unravel the constrictor knot that was now her twisted intestines.

She had so much to consider but, as hard as she tried to push them away, the words *I didn't want this* and *This isn't what I want* rolled around her brain. Yet again, she'd found herself in a situation she hadn't chosen.

She was starting to think that her face was printed on Fate's personal dartboard.

Dodi walked back to the chair she'd used and bent down to pick her large tote off the floor. She pulled it over her shoulder and forced herself to look at Jago. He wore his usual implacable expression, and she couldn't read any emotion in his eyes. 'Sorry, barging in here was a mistake. I should go.'

'Sit down, Elodie Kate.'

She glared at him, ignored him and turned to make her way to the door. She couldn't do this, not now. She needed time to think, to plan, to consider her options. Space.

'I swear, if you leave I will follow you, pick you up, toss you over my shoulder and bring you back here,' Jago stated, his voice calm but determined.

Dodi whirled around to face him, her mouth falling open at his ridiculous statement. 'You wouldn't dare!'

'Try me and see,' Jago softly replied. His low tone and determined expression convinced her there was a better than excellent chance of him doing exactly that.

'Sit down, Dodi, and tell me why you are here.'

Dodi tapped her foot and looked past him to the huge seascape on the wall behind his desk, feeling as if she was tumbling in those waves crashing onto the shore. She couldn't breathe. It was all too much. Why did this always happen to her? Why did her life tend to skid sideways? What was she doing wrong?

Dodi felt the room sway and dots appeared behind her eyes. Her throat started to close. God, was she having a panic attack? If so, she didn't want to have one in front of the imperturbable Jago Le Roux.

A strong hand on her shoulder pushed her down and her bottom hit the seat of a chair. Jago's big hand forced her head to her knees and his rough voice commanded her to take big breaths, slow and deep. After a couple of minutes—years?—her chest and throat loosened. Dodi slowly lifted her head and speared her fingers into her hair, holding her pounding head.

'I swear to God, if you don't tell me what's wrong with you, I'm going to call an ambulance and have you hauled off to the emergency room to be checked over.' She didn't doubt he'd do exactly that.

'I was at my doctor's this morning,' she told him, her voice raspier than usual.

'And? What's the problem? Are you ill?'

Was that a hint of worry she heard in his growly voice or was she imagining it? No, he was just frustrated she was wasting his precious time. Annoyed at him and irritated at herself, she lifted her head to see him leaning his butt against the edge of the desk, his feet crossed at the ankles. His suit trousers brushed her bare knee and she wished she could touch him, just to anchor herself as she delivered her conversational hand grenade.

She could put this off and tell him later…

No, she had to tell him some time and it might as well be now. Dodi pulled in a deep breath, forced her eyes to his face and rubbed the back of her neck.

'I don't know how it happened because we used condoms, except for that one brief moment, but… I'm pregnant. And the baby is yours.'

A heavy, tense, painful silence dropped between them. Jago didn't pull his eyes off her face, neither did his expression change, but she sensed that every muscle in his body contracted, that a nuclear bomb had just been detonated in the depths of his soul.

She started to speak, but before she could she heard a faint buzzing noise.

He grimaced. 'Hold on, my PA needs me.' He issued a voice command to open his intercom system and a few seconds later his PA's voice came through on hidden surround-sound speakers. 'Your investors are downstairs, Mr Le Roux. They'll be here in three minutes.'

Without dropping his eyes from hers, Jago spoke again. 'Put them in the conference room and tell them I'll be a few minutes late.'

He issued another command to mute their conversation, ran his hand through his hair and shook his head, looking only mildly harassed.

Nobody would ever guess that she'd just told him he was about to become a father, that their impulsive one-night stand had resulted in a great big 'oops'. He jammed his hands into the pockets of his trousers and stared at her, his gaze shuttered. Jago was so good at hiding his emotions and she couldn't tell if he was sad or mad, flummoxed or resigned.

She couldn't read him, and a little part of her loathed him for being able to conceal his emotions so well. In contrast, her face was the emotional equivalent of Times Square.

Jago, after many minutes of contemplation, spoke again. 'Are you planning on keeping the baby?'

Dodi threw her hands up in the air. 'I heard I was pregnant a little over an hour ago—I'm still coming to terms with the idea!'

'But you came here, to me, straight away.'

Why had she done that? Why had she run to him? She should've gone home, taken some time to let the news settle, to make sense of this three-sixty turn her life had taken. But her need to see Jago, to share this moment and news with him, had been overwhelming.

'I have no idea what I'm doing, feeling, to be honest. This is all a bit surreal.'

Jago touched his tie, started to pull it down and dropped his hand. Did he need air? She sure did.

Another buzz, followed by the words, 'Sir, you are now more than a few minutes late.'

Jago grimaced at the admonishment coming from the hidden speakers and stood up to walk around the back of his desk. He pulled on his jacket, ran his hand over his head and looked at Dodi from his great height. He gestured to the door. 'I'm sorry but I have to go. This is important.'

And having his baby wasn't? *Seriously?*

Dodi placed her hand on her sternum, trying to physically push back the rolling wave of pain and disappointment. She hadn't expected him to jump for joy, for him to take her in his arms and hold her close—she wasn't that much of a fool!—but she hadn't expected to be dismissed a few minutes after dropping her bombshell news.

And in that instant she was a child again, desperately waiting for her parents to see her, to acknowledge her, to interact with her. To pay her some attention, *any* attention. Then, like now, she'd been treated as an afterthought, a pesky fly that could be ignored, waved away. She wasn't anyone's priority and was of little, or no, importance.

She'd lived with self-involved parents, and after watching her grandmother die had broken up with her long-term boyfriend when she was informed he'd been pathologically unfaithful and emotionally manipulative. She'd experienced grief and loss, heartbreak and betrayal, but she'd never felt as alone as she did right now.

And there was nothing she could do to change it. Dodi pulled in a deep breath, straightened her shoulders, and planted her feet on the floor. Pulling her bag over her shoulder, she stood up, feeling her thick hair falling out of its hastily pinned bun.

Jago placed his hand on her lower back, physically encouraging her to head for the door. She flinched, pulled away from him and quickened her pace. His arm shot past her to open the door and she didn't bother to thank him, choosing instead to walk out of his life with her head held high and her back straight.

'I'll call you later and we can discuss this further,' Jago murmured in her ear.

'You now know, so there's nothing more to discuss.' This was her baby, her body, her life. Had he had anything but a calm, unemotional, almost non-reaction she would've agreed to another discussion, to try and find a way forward together. But because he'd been so damn robotic, practically uninterested, she knew she, and the baby, were problems to be solved, an obstacle to overcome.

Well, at least she knew where she stood. She was on her own.

And that was okay. Being alone, being independent, was what she did. The essence of the person she was.

Hours later, Jago sat on the expansive deck overlooking a waterhole within a private game reserve on the outskirts of Muldersdrift. He tipped his beer bottle to his lips and listened to the shrill song of the cicadas, interspersed with the occasional croak of a bullfrog. The sun was sinking behind the acacia trees, and he heard a group of laughing guests heading towards the open-top game-drive vehicle which stood outside the pub. The place would be quiet for a while—exactly what he needed.

He needed to think, dammit.

After the meeting with his investors finished, he'd driven out to this extensive property, forty minutes northwest of the city, windows down and hoping the hot air would blow the cobwebs from his groggy mind. He owned a half-share in this five-star boutique safari lodge and came here, as often as he could, to this place where the air was clean, the traffic minimal and the birds, animals and insects were frequently his only company. This was his thinking place, a spot with no mobile-phone reception and where he couldn't be disturbed. After taking a beer from the bartender, he had found the most isolated, out-of-the-way corner of the deck and propped his feet up on the railing, desperate to make sense of his suddenly topsy-turvy world.

He leaned back in his chair and tipped his head up to look at the bright stars appearing in the purple-blue, velvety sky. It was past seven and he was exhausted. Physically and mentally drained.

He guessed that was a natural outcome of splitting your thoughts and attention between a complicated business deal and imminent fatherhood. Business was easy…

He'd been working on acquiring a platinum mine

for more than eight months, one of the biggest in the world, but he couldn't leverage enough funding for Le Roux International to buy the mine without partners. Few people in the world could. So he'd looked around for investors, found businessmen he knew and trusted, and pitched his idea. He could've easily postponed the meeting this afternoon, citing a personal emergency, and his colleagues would've understood.

But, feeling sideswiped and off-balance, not knowing how to respond to Dodi's declaration and close to panic, he'd turned to work, something he could control.

But he was done with work and meetings and had run out of excuses, so he had to face Dodi's out-of-the-blue announcement.

She was *pregnant*. The baby was *his*.

Jago stood up and walked along the wooden deck, noticing but not paying any attention to the two kudu bulls approaching the waterhole for an evening drink.

He had not seen this coming. At all.

Anticipating trouble—change—was what he did, who he was. He planned his life, every detail, and he didn't allow life to throw him curveballs. Fathering a child wasn't a curveball, it was a goddamn asteroid strike.

A baby had never been part of the plan. With his wife or anyone else.

His marriage to Anju had been a head decision—he'd liked her mind, they'd both had fun in bed, they'd both agreed love was a myth—and her wish to remain childless and pursue her career had been a stance he fully supported. She'd understood the Le Roux empire required an enormous amount of his time, and neither of them had envisaged his changing nappies while negotiating multi-billion-dollar deals.

But his reluctance to be a dad went deeper than that. He knew himself well, and he was too controlling and analytical to be a father. Because of his need to anticipate trouble, change and potential emotional comet strikes, he constantly scanned his environment, overanalysing and overthinking. He put up barriers, rearranged situations, and either ignored or manoeuvred people to make life easier.

For him.

Children deserved, demanded, and required a father who could engage with, relate to and talk to them, not someone who was rigid and dogmatic, someone who'd stifle their creativity and enthusiasm. He was skilled in many facets of business but being a dad, raising a child, wasn't something he knew how to do. He wouldn't even know where to start and he could see himself screwing up. Badly. To Jago, failure, of any type, was unacceptable.

And frightening.

Children also required emotional availability and he wasn't that type of guy. Smothering his feelings, pushing down his expectations of people, keeping a solid emotional distance between himself and the world had been his coping strategy since he was a child, a way to deal with the vagaries, temper and instability of a volatile father. Hardening his heart was also the only way he could cope with his father's quick remarriage, and the way he'd erased his first wife from his heart, his memories and his life.

Being emotionally distant was a habit now, something he was familiar, and comfortable, with. Something he had no intention of changing…

Except that he had a baby on the way. *Madness.*

But also, weirdly, a little exciting, in an 'I'm about to bungee jump and I don't know if the rope will hold me' type of way. There was a little person on the way who would, at some point, call him Dad. Did he, would he, deserve that title?

And while he was on the subject of questions he couldn't answer, how the hell had Dodi fallen pregnant? As she said, they'd used condoms, every time they made love that night. Hadn't they? Yes, he was pretty sure…

Jago stopped pacing and frowned. He recalled their passion, her frantic demands for him to come into her, and he'd done as she asked, sliding inside her, just once, without being covered because he'd needed to know how she felt without the barrier of latex between them. But he'd pulled out before he'd come, of that he was sure. Had that tiny contact resulted in a child? Could something so life-changing be the result of his need for there to be no barriers between them, just for a minute or two?

Could life be so capricious?

And wasn't that a stupid question? He knew, from experience, exactly how unpredictable life, and people, could be.

And talking about unpredictable, he needed to get

back to the city and face the woman who'd turned his world inside out. They had plans and decisions to make.

Lives to reorganise.

CHAPTER SIX

DODI PULLED HER T-shirt off, pushed down the band of her leggings and stood in front of her free-standing mirror to stare at her still flat stomach. She turned sideways but, as far as she could tell, her breasts weren't any bigger or her stomach any rounder.

She laughed at herself, remembering she was only a few weeks pregnant. Her baby couldn't be bigger than a full stop, less than one millimetre in length, and weighing less than a gram. She'd only start picking up weight in a couple of months and it would be a long time before she felt her baby move.

Her baby.

Emotions, dark and light, battered her from all sides, a constantly changing flow of happy and sad, fear and excitement. Anxiety and anticipation. She was going to be a mum. She was growing a little human she could love. Was she good enough to be a mum? Could she do this on her own?

As a child she'd imagined having a family, being someone's mother, but she'd pushed aside those dreams to focus her attention on how to navigate life with uninterested parents. She'd thought she might, some time in the future, have kids with Dan. But Lily's death, Dan's infidelity, her single status, and the responsibility of running a business had pushed any thoughts of motherhood away. Over the past few years, becoming a parent wasn't something she'd considered. Now it was all she could think about…

Dodi looked at her fingers resting lightly on her stomach, knowing that she was looking for a physical connection to the tiny, tiny human developing inside her. The one she and Jago had made. How she still wasn't sure, but if this kid could fight his or her way past condoms, punch through their protection, she thought the little speck had earned its right to be here, to make its way onto this crazy planet.

And yeah, its father was an unemotional jerk, easily able to brush her and The Speck away, but she couldn't do the same. Wouldn't.

She was keeping this baby…

Excitement and terror gave way to red-hot anger. And all of it was directed at her baby's DNA donor. How dared Jago blow her off, give her life-changing announcement no more attention than he would a memo that crossed his desk? His priority had been his imminent meeting. Hers had *only* been the rest of her life.

She wanted to strangle him…

For being so cool, so unaffected…for transporting her back to her childhood when nothing she said or did resonated with her parents. She'd brought home brilliant report cards. They didn't care. She was hauled into the principal's office—not her fault!—and they'd never bothered to respond to her request for a meeting. They'd shipped her off to live with a stranger…

If she hadn't gone to live with Lily, she might've grown up thinking that her life with her parents was normal, that all mums and dads were uninterested and that kids were supposed to raise themselves. But Lily's deep interest in every facet of her life—her achievements but also her feelings—only highlighted what dreadful parents they were, how much love she'd missed out on. Was it any wonder that she'd fallen into Dan's arms? She'd been a needy, lonely schoolgirl, so empty of love. And he'd been so attentive.

Was she repeating her past mistakes?

Had she slept with Jago because she was lonely, looking for a connection, needing to feel as if she mattered to someone? Oh, of course she mattered to Thadie, but she was, naturally, low on her list of priorities right now. Thadie had the twins, Clyde, a wedding to plan, a new life to embrace. They'd always be friends but her boys, and Clyde, would always come first.

A small part of her, the piece that wasn't cynical and untrusting, wanted to be someone's beginning and end, have their complete attention, be the focus of their interest. Dodi sighed, reluctantly admitting that she'd had that with Jago. For one night she'd been the object of Jago's intense focus, and she'd loved it. But one night had led to enormous consequences…

But not all consequences were terrible. Okay, she was super-angry that she hadn't *chosen* to fall pregnant, but, on the other hand, this baby would be the one person who'd be fully hers, someone who couldn't leave or be taken away, someone she could safely love with all her heart.

She and The Speck would be a team…

And she didn't need Mr 'Nothing Rocks My Boat' Le Roux.

As a single parent, she could control her world, her Speck's world and keep them safe, emotionally as well as physically. By calling the shots, she would always know the ground beneath her was stable, that she wouldn't be forced, manoeuvred, or negotiated into a situation she didn't choose or feel comfortable in. She could work with that…

Dodi heard the chime of her gate's intercom and cocked her head, frowning. She looked at her watch. It was past ten—who on earth would be visiting her?

Jago. It had to be. He was the only person arrogant enough to ring her doorbell nearly half a day after being a cool, dismissive arse.

Picking up her white T-shirt, she walked into the passage, pulled it on and stopped by the stairs to look at the security screen attached to the wall. Yep, that was his swanky car parked in front of their communal boom gate. She swiped the screen to give her a view of the camera pointed at the driver's seat and could see his tense, scowling face.

Dodi watched as he ran a hand across his eyes, pushed it through his short hair. He looked as shattered as she felt…

His hand came out of the car to push the button again and Dodi jumped. He looked directly into the camera, somehow sensing she was watching him.

Dodi picked up the receiver. 'That was a long meeting, Le Roux,' she told him, not bothering with a greeting.

'Let me in, Elodie Kate.'

When hell froze over. 'It's late. Go away.'

He didn't drop his gaze from the camera, and even though the feed was black and white she caught the irritation in his eyes. 'I can sit here all night with my finger on this buzzer. We can do it now or at four in the morning, your choice, but I'm not leaving until we talk.'

Dodi didn't doubt his words. She knew how determined the man could be. He never gave up and he never backed down so, yeah, he'd stay there until she either called the police or her neighbours did, or she let him in.

She cursed and spoke again. 'I'm number ten in the complex. Go right, right again, and left. I'm at the top of the hill.' She slammed the phone down, hit the button to raise the barrier and rested her forehead against the cool wall at the top of the stairs.

The man was infuriating. Sexy as hell but simply exasperating. And, dammit, irresistible.

There was something magical about a single woman's house, Jago decided as he stepped into Dodi's small hallway. That element of enchantment had something to do with the feminine scents that hit his nose, a combination of her perfume, laundry softener and hand-picked roses in a fat glass jar.

Removing his phone from the pocket of his trousers, he placed it, and his car keys, on the small table in the hall and followed Dodi into a vibrantly colourful room. The walls were a rouge pink, the L-shaped sofas a bold blue, and mismatched prints of flowers and figures covered the main wall. Six, no, seven clay-fired pots held luscious plants and the room led into a small conservatory holding a small wooden desk and sixties-style chair. Nothing matched, everything clashed, but it worked. It shouldn't but it did.

'Let's sit outside,' Dodi said, leading him through her conservatory and onto a small outside deck. She gestured to a small wrought-iron table painted in a bold shade of tangerine and rocked on her feet, obviously uncomfortable. Or annoyed. Or a combination of both.

Frankly, he didn't blame her. He'd reacted badly earlier, and he'd barged in here tonight.

'Got anything to drink?' he asked, keeping his tone mild. 'I think this conversation calls for alcohol.'

Politeness warred with fury, but she eventually wrinkled her nose. 'White wine? A light beer?'

'Wine will work.'

Dodi nodded and spun around on her pretty bare feet to walk back into her house. He watched her slim form until she disappeared into the house, thinking that she had the perfect figure to wear tight leggings. Rounded hips and butt, flat stomach, long, long legs. Then he recalled those legs wrapping around his hips, and her breathy moans and how she had dug her nails into the base of his spine.

But their mutual delight and pleasure—he was in no doubt that she'd enjoyed their time in bed as much as he had—resulted in her falling pregnant, and that was what he had to focus his attention on. Not her lovely breasts under that tight white cropped T-shirt, or his quest to discover where else she had delightful freckles…

Dodi placed a bottle of white wine, glistening with condensation, on the table and handed him a wine glass. Lifting the bottle, she started to dash some into her glass before pulling a face.

'Problem?' he asked.

She nodded. 'Being pregnant, I shouldn't be drinking alcohol…'

He was desperate for the soothing effects of the fermented grape, but if she had to have this conversation sober then so should he. He pushed the wine bottle back into her hand, asked for a glass of water and tried not to think about the case of Domaine de la Romanée-Conti he'd received just yesterday. Rare and fabulous in contrast to the fruity combination of chemicals Dodi had just offered.

She went back inside to get his water and he wondered if he was turning into a snob. No, thanks to a lifetime of privilege, he'd probably always been one. He'd grown up as a child of extreme wealth and was used to the best money could buy. His father had many faults, but Theo had worked hard and insisted they did too, at school, university and then in the business. Theo hadn't made any allowances for his sons—if anything, he was a lot harder on them than on his other employees.

There was one element of his father's life that Jago wouldn't emulate: he'd vowed not to have children. He refused to inflict another generation with a screwed-up father.

But one tiny mistake, one impulsive action had

led to the creation of life, and he'd been, without any warning, promoted to being a trainee father. He wasn't ready, didn't want the responsibility. Was scared to his soul.

Jago rubbed his hands over his face and when he dropped them he looked at Dodi, who sat down opposite him.

For the first time in what had to be years, decades, he didn't know what to say, how to act. What to think. He felt as if he was standing in a dense web, unable to think, breathe, speak. What was the next step? Where did they go from here?

Dodi broke their tense silence. 'Why are you here, Jago? You made your feelings very clear this morning when you hustled me out of your office.'

He hadn't known what to think, had still been processing her news, trying to understand, so there had been no feelings to transmit. He'd still been trying to wrap his head around her grenade-exploding news. He frowned. 'I didn't say anything,' he protested.

'Exactly!' Dodi hotly replied. 'I told you I'm pregnant with your child and you told me that you had a meeting. Hell, Jago, that reaction would've made a robot proud!'

He was robotic? Her words were a whip slicing across his soul. He was aloof, distant, standoffish but he hadn't always been that way. As a child, he'd been more communicative, quick to laugh, to have fun. To give and receive affection. But after his mum's death he'd started to retreat from people, made sure to keep his distance, and made it a habit to scan the horizon for potential emotional traps.

Drama—verbal, physical, emotional—had become something to avoid.

Dodi closed her eyes, took a deep breath and linked her hands across her flat stomach. 'Finish your water, walk out of my house and out of my life. Neither of us needs you.'

He lowered his glass. Had he heard her properly? 'I'm sorry?'

Dodi rubbed her forehead with the pads of her index finger and thumb. 'I'm going to keep this baby, Jago, but that's my choice. I can afford to be a single mother, to give this baby everything it needs. We agreed to a one-night stand and I'm not looking for more. Go back to your normal life and pretend this never happened.'

What. The. Hell.

She couldn't possibly think that he'd stroll out and leave her, well, literally holding the baby. He knew he had a reputation for being ruthless, driven and obsessed when it came to his family and Le Roux International, but he also took full responsibility for his actions. And he certainly wasn't going to allow her to dictate the terms of this strange situation, to kick him out of her and his baby's life.

She was the mother of his child, and he was tied to her, in a fundamental way, for the rest of his life.

He swallowed some hot words and hauled in some air. 'There's no way in hell that's going to happen.'

'You only wanted a one-night stand, so I'm not stupid enough to believe that you suddenly want to play daddy.' Dodi narrowed her eyes, now as cold as a Highveld winter's morning.

He'd never wanted children so he couldn't argue with her reasoning. 'True enough.'

'Well, then, for God's sake, go! I'm giving you permission to walk!' Dodi cried, her voice rising with frustration.

Jago felt his temper bubble. 'Firstly, I don't need your permission to do anything. Secondly, there's another option.' He needed to have her close, for how else would he be able to protect her from anything ugly heading her way? Like Micah and Thadie, she and his child were now under his protection. How could he do that if he wasn't close by?

'What? Are you going to tell me we should get married?' she asked him, her expression mocking.

The thought was initially, just for a few seconds, jarring.

'Yes.'

The axis holding the earth in place shook and he wondered what entity had taken control of his mouth. He'd never intended to marry again or planned on having a child, but once his shock had receded the thought, surprisingly, didn't scare him.

Or didn't scare him as much as he thought it *should*.

He sent her a steady look. 'We're *going* to get married, you're *going* to move into Hadleigh House, and we're *going* to raise this child together.'

Her mouth dropped open and her eyes clouded over with confusion. He waited for his words to register and when they did, instead of blasting him, she released a belly laugh. 'Oh, that's too funny.'

Really? Strange, but he couldn't find anything amusing about their current situation. Was he missing something here?

* * *

As she took in Jago's thundercloud face, Dodi's laughter faded away. God, he was being serious! He actually expected her to marry him, after just a few conversations and a night spent in his bed.

What an insane idea!

Having witnessed her parents' lackadaisical approach to marriage and commitment, and knowing the detrimental effect it had on her, Dodi took the idea of being legally and morally linked to another person extremely seriously. Marriage was a commitment that should be separate from pregnancy, and one shouldn't influence the other. Outside forces or circumstances shouldn't play a part in any decision to commit to spending the rest of their lives together. She'd been a 'mistake', an unwanted pregnancy, and her parents had married because they'd thought it the right thing to do…

It hadn't been, not for them and not for her.

And what was Jago thinking with his 'going' to do this, and 'going' to do that statements? She was not *going* to allow him to push her into a relationship, house or situation she didn't want to be in, one she hadn't chosen. She was a grown adult, perfectly able to make her own decisions, one who didn't need a man to support, protect or dominate her.

Who did he think he was?

Exasperation, impatience and fury sparked her temper to life. Standing up, she stomped over to the French doors and gestured for him to leave. When he didn't move, she forced the words past her gritted teeth. 'Get out.'

Jago folded his arms across his broad chest, stubbornness turning his eyes to the colour and texture of slate. 'No. We're talking about this.'

'We're not talking, you're dictating!' Dodi shouted at him, vibrating with outrage. 'That might work at Le Roux International, but it won't with me! I am not one of your employees and you don't get to tell me what to do!'

She clenched her fists, her nails biting into her palms. Stomping back over to the table, she placed her hands flat on the surface and leaned forward, bending her head to stare into Jago's eyes. 'You are *not* the boss of me.'

Blue and grey eyes clashed and held. Jago eventually broke their stare by rubbing his hand down his face, across his mouth and briefly closing his eyes. He sat back, breathed deeply and Dodi knew that he was trying to harness his temper.

Maybe she should do the same. Standing up straight, she paced the small area of her deck before turning her back on him and looking to the small water fountain in the corner of her enclosed yard. The pretty garden, overlooked by a memorial plaque she'd put up for Lily on the back wall, looked ragged and overgrown. She hadn't tended the garden for weeks and her fingers itched to dig in the soil, to pull out weeds, to tidy it up. To restore a little bit of order to her chaotic world.

Feeling a smidgeon calmer, Dodi turned back to Jago and rocked on her heels.

'This could be so much worse, you know,' she told him.

He looked at her in disbelief. 'It could? How?'

'I could be a teenager, with absolutely no resources, pregnant by a boy who didn't have a job, couldn't be bothered to find one, couldn't be bothered about me or the baby. I could be a mum with four kids to feed, with no money to raise another. But I'm a wealthy, privileged woman, who has the money to raise this child on my own. I'm healthy, I have a house, I have medical. I own my own business and have fabulous staff, so I can pick and choose the times I go to work and take the baby with me when I do.'

'You seem to have it all worked out,' Jago stated with an edge to his voice. 'What do you want from me?'

'Right at this moment, I don't want or need anything from you, Jago,' Dodi quietly told him. 'I don't need you to rush in and rescue me, to marry me or do anything equally stupid. I've been on my own for a long time and I'm perfectly happy to walk this path alone.'

She read the expression on his face as clearly as if he'd spoken: that's not going to happen. Dodi rubbed the back of her neck, exhausted. She didn't want to argue any more. 'Look, if you want to claim this baby as yours, you can put your name on the birth certificate. If you want to see the child, have him, or her be part of your life, we can talk about that…visitation rights, et cetera. But I'm not forcing you to be, or do, anything that makes you feel uncomfortable. I expect you to treat me the same way.'

'That's all very well, Elodie Kate, but you have the right to ask me to step up to the plate, to take responsibility and to play my part. I was there. You didn't get pregnant on your own!'

He was overbearing and bossy and was used to getting his way, but he was, in his screwed-up way, trying to be the good guy, to do the right thing. She had to respect that. Then she caught the flash of determination in his eyes and knew that he wasn't backing down, he was just trying to find another way to get what he wanted. Not going to happen, bud.

'You are thinking that you will work around me, to manoeuvre me into, at the very least, moving in with you.'

He didn't deny her accusation. 'I live in a huge house with servants, a massive garden, a pool and a gym. Your meals will be cooked for you, your laundry and cleaning done. At Hadleigh House, you'd be looked after, by me and my staff.'

'I don't need to be looked after!' Dodi wailed. 'That's not your job!'

God, how was she going to get through to him?

'Jago, you are very used to getting your way,' Dodi told him, her voice taking on a hard edge. 'But I am not your brother, sister or one of your many responsibilities. Yes, I'm pregnant, with your child, but that doesn't mean you get to swoop in and start arranging my life.'

She walked over to the French doors and waited as he followed her to his feet. 'Don't make decisions for me. I don't want you to, and I don't need you to. If you decide to be part of this baby's life, I will discuss that. But I will not be dictated to, manipulated or manoeuvred.'

Dodi rocked on her heels, feeling like a battery that

was drained of power. 'I need you to go, Jago. It's been a long, long, emotional day and I'm wiped.'

'We'll talk soon,' Jago said, nodding. 'Hopefully we'll make more progress next time.'

He wasn't backing down or giving up. God help her. Jago surprised her when he lowered his head to place his lips against her temple. 'Call me if you need me, Elodie Kate.'

Dodi stepped back and looked up. 'I make it a point of never needing anybody for anything,' she informed him.

He brushed his thumb over her cheek and Dodi fought the urge to step into his arms and seek his warmth and strength. 'Start thinking of what you want to be moved into Hadleigh House, sweetheart. And as soon as you give me the word, I'll send the movers to pack up your stuff.'

'I am not—' Dodi bit off the words and pointed in the direction of the front door. 'Out! Now!'

Luckily, this time he listened. Dodi didn't expect him to do it again.

CHAPTER SEVEN

SHORTLY BEFORE LUNCH the next day Jago slipped into Love & Enchantment unnoticed. The place was packed to the gills with prospective brides, bridesmaids, family members and the odd male hanging around looking uncomfortable.

His eyebrows rose as a slim, willowy blonde walked out from the dressing rooms in a strip of feathers covering her breasts and her hips. It was white, so he assumed it was a wedding dress. Look, he wasn't a prude, but surely a wedding dress required a little more fabric?

And God, he hoped the priest, the groom or the best man didn't have any heart issues, because they'd need a defibrillator when they saw that…*thing*…she was *almost* wearing.

Jago stepped to the side, hid behind an enormous bouquet of white lilies, happy to watch the mayhem. A pretty girl across the room stared at her meringue-like dress in the mirror, swishing her skirts as a four-year-old would.

A Goth-looking bride—black-as-coal hair and even blacker lipstick—stepped up onto a dais and cocked her head to look at the Morticia Adams-style wedding dress. Black, of course.

Her voice drifted over to Jago. 'Could I wear a witch's hat?'

Honestly, he thought she should. The dress certainly called for it.

Jago leaned his shoulder into the wall. This was actually fun. The customers seemed to be enjoying the experience and Dodi's staff appeared relaxed and efficient and had perpetual smiles on their faces. And yeah, he was happy to stand here as he worked out how to apologise to Dodi. Apologies weren't something he often did, and he sucked at them.

But he'd properly screwed up last night. He'd been tired and wired, upset and off-balance, and that made him rude. He should've taken some time to decompress and think before confronting Dodi.

And what had he been thinking when he demanded that she marry him or, at the very least, move in with him? He had a lot more finesse than that. He still wanted her living at Hadleigh House, sharing his bed, but her back was up and he'd have to work twice as hard to get her there.

He genuinely thought that moving in with him—he conceded that mentioning marriage had been a step too far—was a reasonable, sensible option. She was pregnant, owned a business and lived alone. And, being as independent as she was, she found it hard to ask for help, he suspected. He had the money, power and resources to make her life easier, to smooth away the obstacles that made life difficult and tiresome.

It was for her own good…hers and the baby's.

But he'd have to tread carefully. Dodi wasn't a pushover and had more pride than most.

Jago's eyes moved around the room and his heart kicked up when he saw Dodi walking into the salon from the staff area, a fixed smile on her face. In her white silk T-shirt tucked into wide-legged trousers, she looked professional and sophisticated, but under her pleasant expression he could detect her frustration.

Something was wrong. He knew it the way he knew Hadleigh House.

As if sensing him, she jerked her chin up and looked around, immediately zeroing in on him standing in the corner. Those perfect, russet eyebrows lifted, silently asking why he was standing in her salon on a Friday afternoon, one of the busiest afternoons of the week.

Handing the dresses she carried to an assistant, she crossed the room to him. Standing close to him, she tipped her head to the side. 'What are you doing here, Jago?'

He couldn't tell her that their situation was all he could think about. And they weren't just thoughts about the baby, but also thoughts of *her.* What she tasted like, how she smelled, how he felt as if he was home when her arms wrapped around him, connected to her body. How much he wanted to be with her again, making love or just talking. He didn't care which.

'I need to apologise for my behaviour last night,' he quietly stated.

She waited, her eyebrows still raised. He rubbed the back of his neck. 'I'm sorry, I was out of line.'

She nodded. 'You were. Apology accepted.'

That was it? Two words? He frowned, unsure of

her brief response. Did she mean it? 'Let me take you to lunch so I can apologise properly.'

'You just did, and I really can't.' Dodi gestured to the packed room and shook her head. 'It's crazy busy, Jago, as you can see. I'm not going anywhere, not for a while yet.'

Now that he was here, he desperately wanted to spend some time with her. He glanced at his watch. 'How long until the madness dies down?'

'An hour, maybe two?' Dodi replied before shaking her head. 'But I can't leave the premises today. I have so much to do.'

'It's Friday, Elodie Kate, and work will still be there on Monday.'

Dodi reached up to lay the back of her hand against his brow, his cheek. 'Are you feeling okay? Who are you and what have you done with Jago Le Roux, the workaholic?'

'Funny.'

'I thought it was,' Dodi told him, a small smile touching her sexy mouth.

'That dress looks like a bowl of cat sick,' a female voice stated.

Dodi widened her eyes at Jago before turning to look around at the group closest to them. Three women stood in front of a cross-looking blonde woman, sitting back in the chair as if she were a young queen, disdain on her face. It was obvious to Jago that she held the power in the group and had every intention of wielding it.

Jago fought the urge to bolt for the door. He didn't belong here. Weddings, love, frippery and fancies weren't his thing. But he still wanted to take Dodi to lunch, get some food in her. She was looking too thin and a little washed out.

Was she taking vitamins? Getting enough sleep? Looking after herself? He needed to know…

But only because she was having his baby.

Lying to yourself now, Le Roux? That was a new low.

'I hate my job,' Dodi whispered, seemingly to herself.

Jago looked down at her and saw the truth of that statement reflected in her face. She looked as if she'd rather be anywhere but here…

But why? Surely not because some drama queen was being nasty to one of her bridal party? This should be a happy place to work, with people wanting to be pleased, enjoying the experience, content to spend money on their fairy-tale dress. But Dodi wasn't as enamoured with running the shop as everyone thought. Interesting.

Then again, everything was interesting about this woman. And that was…interesting in a terrifying kind of way.

Dodi left his side, bent over the shoulder of the bridezilla and murmured in her ear. The woman shot up, spun around and slowly stood up, her eyes wide. She followed Dodi over to a quiet corner and, with Dodi's back to him, he watched her face pale, flush and pale again. Then her shoulders slumped, and she stared at her feet, her expression now miserable.

Right, there was no doubt that Dodi had just informed her that bitchiness was not permitted in her salon. Good for her.

Dodi and the bride-to-be walked back towards him and the group. 'Ladies, Dana would like to take you all to lunch and then, after you've had something to eat, we'll resume the appointment. Is that okay with you?'

The three women looked at the prospective bride. Her bottom lip wobbled, and a tear slid down her face. 'I'm sorry but I miss my mum and I just want her here!'

The bride opened her arms and the group huddled together, laughing and crying. Dodi rolled her eyes at Jago and, taking his hand, pulled him back to the entrance of her salon. 'Drama, drama, more drama. It never stops!'

'You certainly talked the Bridezilla around.'

'She's young, scared, missing her mum and desperately hoping that a lovely wedding will make her feel happy again. That her boyfriend will provide the happiness she so desperately craves,' Dodi replied, with a bite in her voice.

'Wow, cynical.'

'No, truthful. Other people—friends, lovers, husbands—can't make you happy. A person has to make their own happiness.'

Jago looked around the room before connecting with her smoke-blue gaze again. 'And this doesn't make you happy?'

She stared at him, moved from foot to foot and dropped her gaze, as if she was trying to find a way to avoid his question. Her shoulders lifted to her ears and stayed there. 'No, it doesn't, not particularly.'

Dodi reached around him and opened her front door. 'Thanks for stopping by and the offer of lunch. But as you can see, I have fires to put out.'

He smiled at her. 'Don't make any more brides cry.'

'I'll try not to.' Her smile turned brighter. 'Although someone—a father, fiancé or the bride herself—might weep when I present them with the bill.'

He smiled, enchanted by her. 'I'll pick you up here at six, take you for an early meal.'

'I can't, it's—'

He cut off her words by dropping a kiss on her nose. 'Six o'clock. Be ready.'

He felt her eyes boring into his back but didn't turn around to look at her. If he did, he might be tempted to take her into his arms and kiss her senseless.

Not what her clients needed to see on a sunny, late summer day.

The only reason she was going out for an early meal with the very high-handed Jago was that she was starving—she'd missed lunch—and because she didn't have any food in the house. And, even if she had, she didn't have the energy to cook it.

Sliding into his car, something stupidly low and ridiculously expensive, Dodi pulled her seatbelt across her stomach and clicked it into place. She was only five, nearly six weeks pregnant, but man, the hormones were rocking around her system. She was tired, more exhausted than she ever recalled being in her life, constantly nauseous, and yeah, her patience levels, never good, were running low.

She remembered Jago's offer to look after her, for

her to move into Hadleigh House and to have his butler and staff take care of her. He wanted to wrap her in cotton wool and smooth her path through life. Tonight, she was tempted to let him do that. She was *that* tired and overwhelmed.

'You doing okay?'

Dodi slowly rolled her head in his direction, lifting a hand to smother her yawn. She couldn't let him know that she was feeling vulnerable and emotional, she couldn't give him that much leverage. 'Just tired. It's been a long day, a long week.'

Jago nodded. 'For me too. Let's find a pub, get a drink and, more importantly, some food into you.'

Food, a bath, and an early night. It sounded like bliss. She should work—her paperwork was piling up—but, right now, she didn't care. Dodi, enjoying the light, cooling air coming from the vents, slid down further in the seat and felt her eyelids dropping. She couldn't fall asleep, shouldn't, but it was so nice being in this car. It was a cool, cosy, comfortable cocoon…

Dodi woke up to the sound of a car door closing, the smell of good quality leather and the seatbelt digging across her chest. She blinked, disorientated. Where was she?

She looked out of the front window at the modernistic, L-shaped house with its flat roof and banks of tinted floor-to-ceiling windows, and it took her a minute to recognise the house Jago lived in when he'd been married to Anju. She'd only ever visited once, with Thadie. Anju, she recalled, hadn't invited them in.

So Jago still owned this house. Why hadn't he sold it? And why were they here?

Releasing herself from the seatbelt, she saw Jago talking to a large man wearing body armour, a huge pistol on his hip. Opening her car door, she climbed out and walked over to them, pulling the band to release her falling-down hair.

'What's going on?' she asked, confused. Why were they here and not at the pub? And this house was at least a forty-five-minute drive from her salon…had she been asleep all this time? And why had Jago let her sleep?

She caught his eye, the warmth in his small smile, and felt her heart quiver. She didn't need him looking at her like that. Neither did she need him to be caring and considerate. It both warmed and confused her and, worse, tempted her to let him take over.

Jago gestured to the security guard. 'This is Bheki, from the alarm company. An alarm was triggered here so he asked me to meet him here.'

It took Dodi a moment to connect the dots. 'Someone has broken in?' she asked, moving closer to Jago.

Jago lightly touched her back with the tips of his fingers. 'No, no one is here,' Jago replied. 'It must've been a glitch in the system.'

Bheki nodded. 'I'll get going, then, Mr Le Roux.' He nodded to the open front door behind them. 'Don't forget to lock up.'

'I won't. Thanks.'

Bheki hopped into his response vehicle, reversed and drove away. Jago looked down at Dodi before lifting his hand to run his thumb across her cheekbone. 'Did you have a good nap?'

She blushed. 'I did. I can't remember when last I slept for forty-five minutes.'

He grinned. 'It was closer to an hour, actually.'

'You drove me around for an hour?'

He shrugged. 'You needed sleep, so I gave it to you.'

It was a sweet gesture, considerate and very kind. And very unexpected coming from the terse 'time is money' billionaire.

Jago smiled. 'And you snore, by the way.'

Really? No, she didn't! Needing to change the subject, she gestured to his house. 'I thought you sold this place.'

His expression clouded and he shook his head.

She took a step towards the open door, then stopped. 'Can I look around inside? I remember Thadie raving about the design.' Seeing that he was about to say no, she carried on quickly. 'Just a quick peek, Jago.'

He pulled a face before taking her hand and leading her up the three shallow steps to the oversized front door. 'It hasn't been opened for a while, so it will likely smell musty,' he said, leading her into the two-storey rotunda. The deep grey floors were highly glossy and complemented the light grey walls and a modern floating staircase.

Dodi walked across the rotunda into a massive open-plan living, dining and kitchen area, minimalistic, elegant, and very, very cold with its silver and white accents. She noticed the hand-painted cushions on the sofa and the large and expensive coffee table books stacked neatly on the glass table. It looked like a show house, waiting for its new, wealthy owner to arrive. It didn't look like a house that had stood empty for years.

On the other side of the rotunda was a high-tech media and games room with a huge, wall-mounted TV and a full-sized billiard table. The bi-fold doors opened up onto a long entertainment deck edged by a two-person lap pool. Beyond the pool was a well maintained, manicured garden.

She could see signs of Anju everywhere and it felt as if she'd just left the room. There was a book on neuroplasticity sitting on a side table, a bookmark peeking out from between its covers. There was even a cream cardigan hanging over the back of a chair, something Jago must've missed when he'd packed up the house.

If he'd packed up the house…

'Can I look upstairs?' she asked.

Jago nodded and followed her up the floating stairs to the second floor. To her, it felt as if the house was holding its breath, as if it was full of tension, desperate to exhale. It felt cold and lonely and, despite the slick decor, expensive art and high-end furniture, oozed neglect. Houses needed human energy, and they needed to be lived in.

At the top of the stairs, Dodi turned right and poked her head into three luxurious, huge guest rooms, all with en-suite bathrooms. Hotel rooms, she decided. Moving to the other side of the hall, she opened another door and blinked at the floor-to-ceiling bookshelves containing, well, books, arranged alphabetically. She also noticed a closed laptop, a stack of notebooks, pottery containers holding pens, a stack of folders. A shelf containing files lined the wall above the desk and a corkboard was covered in sticky notes in elegant handwriting, a reminder of appointments and oft used phone numbers.

It looked as if someone, a feminine someone, had just stepped out of the room and had run downstairs for a break.

This was, had to be, Anju's study. But why hadn't Jago cleared it out, packed up her things? Puzzled, Dodi left the study and eyed the room at the end of the hall, deciding whether she should go in or not. It was where Jago and Anju had spent their most intimate moments together and she wasn't sure she wanted to see where they'd loved and, hopefully, laughed.

But she was curious to know whether Jago had cleared this room or whether it was a shrine to his dead wife.

Sucking in a deep breath, she opened the door and slipped inside, her eyes rising at the massive bed that dominated the stark white room. Floor-to-ceiling windows on two sides allowed the light in, but it was so cold and clinical it reminded her of a hospital room. Walking around the back of the bed, she found a bathroom with a huge two-person shower and twin granite basins. Putting her finger on the cupboard below one basin, she pulled it open and saw that the shelves were bare. Unable to stop snooping, she popped open the door under the other basin and saw that it was filled with high-end toiletries and expensive make-up, two-thousand-dollar bottles of perfume.

Jago had cleared out his stuff but not Anju's.

There was a walk-in closet leading off both the bathroom and the bedroom, but Dodi didn't need to look inside it to know that she would find Anju's clothes, her handbags, shoes and accessories.

Biting her lip, she walked back into the bedroom and over to the corner of the room to look down onto the entertainment deck and the landscaped garden. Was Jago in a holding pattern? Had he still not accepted Anju's death? Not moved on? Was he still living in the past?

Dodi heard Jago's footsteps and turned to watch him enter the room. He wore his normal impassive expression but his eyes seemed darker, a little more turbulent.

He joined her at the window and leaned his shoulder into the glass, folding his arms across his wide chest, the fabric of his shirt tight across his big biceps. And Dodi felt that familiar rush of heat, that weird *I want you now* feeling.

Her body wanted his again, over hers, under hers, hot and hard. But her mind was flashing huge red warning lights, telling her to be very, very careful. He was a complicated man, one fighting demons. She had her problems. She didn't want to help him fight his. Not that he would let her. Jago was the most emotionally distant person she'd ever met and wasn't one to invite confidences.

'Do you like the house?' Jago asked her, a slight frown pulling his eyebrows together.

She wished she could say that she did, but she didn't, not at all. Oh, it was innovative and thoughtfully designed, with super-luxurious finishes, but it was cold and stark and every room made her want to pull on a cardigan or wrap her arms around her torso to contain her shiver.

She looked for a diplomatic way to tell him that she didn't.

The corner of Jago's mouth lifted in that sexy almost smile. 'Don't hurt yourself trying to be kind. I can see that you don't.'

Oops. She shrugged. 'I far prefer your family home,' she admitted. 'It's…warmer.'

Dodi walked over to the bed and sat down, crossing one leg over the other. Should she ask him why he hadn't sold the house and cleared out her things? Did she have a right to question him, to pry into his life? No, probably not. They'd only slept together once, had a few conversations. They weren't friends…

But they were also going to have a baby together.

She'd ask. He'd either answer her or not. 'Why haven't you emptied the house, Jago? Packed up Anju's stuff, sold the property? Why leave it?'

His hard eyes slammed into hers and Dodi saw the turbulence within all that grey. He didn't speak and she bit down on her bottom lip, wondering whether to push forward or retreat.

His body language screamed for her to back away, to give him some space, that he wasn't ready to discuss his dead wife with her or, knowing Jago, anyone at all. This was a no-go area, a field pitted with conversational land mines, and Jago was on the other side of the fence.

Safe but still so very wounded.

So why did she want to push him? She had no right to, and she hated it when people tried to do a deep dive into her psyche. She prized her emotional privacy, and she should respect Jago's.

It was only fair.

She stood up abruptly and lifted her hands in a conciliatory gesture. 'I'm sorry, I have no right to pry. It's got nothing to do with me.'

Jago didn't reply and after staring at his still form for a minute she grimaced, then sighed. 'I'll wait for you downstairs and, if it's okay, I think I'll skip dinner. I'm pretty tired.'

Dodi turned to walk out of the room, her heels echoing in the empty space. She was at the door when Jago cleared his throat.

'I didn't want her forgotten. That's why I haven't packed up the house.'

Turning, Dodi put her hands behind her back and rested her open palms on the wall behind her. She looked across the room and saw that Jago had pushed his hands into the pockets of his suit trousers. His shoulders were still raised, and his eyes were filled with emotional whirlpools.

'You must've loved her so very much, Jago. And I'm so sorry you lost her.'

Jago's head snapped up, his expression puzzled. He looked as if he wanted to disagree with her, to tell her that she had it wrong. No, that didn't make sense at all. He'd married Anju, and the few times she saw them together they'd seemed happy in a busy, modern, non-affectionate way.

What was she missing here? 'You did love her, right?' Dodi asked, confused.

Jago shrugged. 'Love never really came up.'

What?

Jago removed the gold cufflinks holding the cuffs of his shirt together at his wrists and shoved them into his pocket, quickly rolling his shirtsleeves up his muscled, tanned arms. His veins under the skin were raised, the way they always were on super-fit guys. Sexy.

Don't get distracted, Dodi.

Jago looked around the room and shrugged. When he spoke again, his voice was rough with pain. 'Within two, three weeks of my mum dying, my dad had the staff pack up everything that was hers, every last thing. He didn't consult us or ask us if there was anything of hers we wanted.'

Dodi's head jerked up, and her lips parted in surprise. Partly because he was opening up, partly because his words were so bizarre.

'Sorry?' she asked, not sure she was hearing him correctly.

His small smile was sour. 'He stripped the house of her, basically eradicated her presence from his life, from our lives. He donated all her clothes to charity, sold her jewellery at a specialised auction, burned her diaries and personal documents.'

Odd, Dodi thought. And so, so sad.

'And six weeks later he was dating Liyana,' Jago said, his voice flat and emotionless. Right, she was beginning to realise that the less emotion there was in his voice, the more deeply ran his emotions.

Jago looked around his old bedroom. 'I suppose that's the real reason I haven't packed up this house. I didn't want Anju forgotten.'

Dodi tipped her head to the side. 'I think that's part of it...but that's not the only reason.'

Jago gripped the bridge of his nose. 'Jesus. How did you figure that out?'

Not having an explanation, Dodi shrugged. He could see below her surface as well. Fair was fair, she thought. 'Will you tell me the other reason you've held on to this house?'

He pushed his hand through his hair. 'Ah...that would be Theo's fault. My father didn't approve of me marrying Anju. He said that I didn't know what I was doing and that I was making a mistake. He refused to help me buy a house and wouldn't let me stay in any of the many rental properties Le Roux International owned. I refused to listen to him, and our relationship, never easy, soured. By marrying, I was defying him, and he was determined to make it as hard as possible for me to do that.

'I used the money my mum left me, took out a huge mortgage and bought and designed this house,' Jago explained. 'It's the only asset I have that's not tied into the complex web that is Le Roux International, that isn't connected, in any way, to the business or the family. It's mine. In every way.'

'And why is that important to you?' Dodi asked.

'It's my back-up plan. If anything, and everything, goes wrong with the business, with us, I have this property to fall back on. I can live in it or leverage it to start something new. I always anticipate trouble, Elodie Kate, and I consider the worst-case scenarios. And then I prepare for them.'

Wow. That was a hell of a way to live. And this had

to be a deep-seated belief because Le Roux International was one of the biggest and most stable companies in the country, on the continent. It would take an event of epic proportions to collapse it.

She could poke holes in his theory but wouldn't. She had no right to. This was his journey to walk, his road to map out, his emotions to walk through.

She wouldn't offer unsolicited advice. She had her hang-ups and issues and couldn't judge his.

'No comment?' Jago asked her.

Dodi shook her head. 'No. Anju was your wife, this is your house, and they are your mental processes.'

She wouldn't judge him. She had her own defences and walls and was still trying to deal with her past—Lily's death and Dan's deceit.

The combination of her parents' craziness and emotional neglect, Lily dying, and Dan's infidelity and mind games made her accept—once and for all—that love was a fairy tale, concocted to sell Valentine's Day cards and chocolates, engagement rings and wedding dresses.

No wonder she felt like such a fraud, owning, working at and making money from Love & Enchantment.

But this discussion wasn't about her, it was about Jago and this house and his past. Dodi forced a smile onto her face and gestured to the door. She wanted out of here and felt a little claustrophobic, her chest tight. 'Shall we go?'

Jago nodded and followed her path to the still-open front door, noticing that dusk had fallen and that the temperature had dropped, from hot as hell to hot. She pushed a tendril of hair behind her ear, thinking that she was due to give birth at the beginning of December, one of the hottest months of the year. Carrying a bowling ball around in that heat wasn't going to be fun.

Jago punched a code into the alarm panel at the front door and locked the door behind him. Placing his hand on Dodi's lower back, he steered her to his car, reaching around her to open the passenger door for her.

In the car, he started the engine, turned the air-conditioning up and they both sighed when cool air hit their faces. Jago flicked on the headlights before turning to face her. 'I asked you to share a meal with me tonight so that we could talk more about the baby, and the future, but we haven't even come close to broaching that subject.'

But she didn't want to, not tonight. She was tired after a long week, and she was taking tomorrow off, leaving the salon in the capable hands of her second-in-command. Tonight, all she wanted was a cup of tea, a shower and to sleep.

'I'm really tired, Jago, and not up for an intense discussion.'

He nodded before expertly reversing his car and pulling away. 'I figured. But we're going to have to talk about it some time, Elodie Kate.'

But not tonight and that was all she cared about.

Jago navigated his way through the suburb and within minutes they were on the freeway, and he was weaving his way through the evening rush-hour traffic. After a few minutes of silence, he spoke again.

'Have you told Thadie, or anyone else, about the baby?'

No, and she did feel guilty about keeping such a huge secret from her best friend. But Thadie had so much on her plate right now. 'I haven't. I don't want my news taking away from what should be Thadie's time and moment. And I think it's sensible to, at the very least, wait until I've seen the heartbeat before I say anything. Most women are told by their doctors to wait until three months have passed before telling anyone, as most miscarriages happen early,' she added.

He sent her a quick but intense look. 'Is miscarrying something you're worried about?'

Dodi shrugged. 'I'm healthy but a lot of healthy women miscarry. Let's wait for the first scan before we say anything. That will happen around eight weeks. If everything is fine at that point, we can talk about telling your family. And maybe we should delay the how-we're-going-to-go-forward conversation until then, as well.'

His family. She didn't have any of her own. God, she missed her grandmother.

She felt his eyes touch her face. 'I'll agree to keep the baby a secret until then but not the conversation. We are going to talk, Dodi, sooner rather than later.'

Ack. Well, she tried.

Jago took the exit that would take her home and stopped at the traffic lights, tapping his finger on his leather-covered steering wheel. 'What are you doing this weekend?' Jago asked her.

'Pottering, mostly. Hopefully, I'll catch up with Thadie and the twins, too.'

'I'm heading to Cape Town tomorrow for a conference. Next weekend?' Jago asked, pulling off.

'Uh…' God, it was embarrassing to admit that her social life was a wasteland. That she spent most weekends catching up on chores or binging series on Netflix. 'Nothing exciting…why?'

'There's a wine and appetiser reception I've been invited to, to raise funds for a cancer research charity, at Moon next Saturday night. Would you like to come with me?'

To Moon? One of the swankiest venues in the city? *Uh...*

It sounded as if Jago was asking her out on a date, that he wanted her with him on the night. But why? They'd just slept together, weren't planning on doing it again and were now—*eek!*—having a baby together. Why was he complicating an already complicated situation by asking her to upmarket events at a luxurious rooftop venue?

Jago placed his hand on her knee and squeezed. 'Stop overthinking this, Dodi. I need a date, and you, I think, need to get out of your head and your house. Come with me, meet some new people, plug your business. God knows there is always a bride or two wafting around looking for their first, second or third wedding dress. You might as well be the one to provide them with what they want.'

He sounded so cynical, Dodi thought. Is that how she sounded about marriage, about weddings? Sceptical and harsh? If yes, then she needed to tone it down a notch or four hundred.

Jago squeezed her knee again and Dodi realised

that he was waiting for her reply. 'Um… I don't know, Jago. We said one night, nothing more.'

'Nothing was written in blood, Dodi, and we can spend an evening together without us ripping each other's clothes off, right?' Well, maybe he could. She wasn't so sure about herself.

'And I'm thinking that, if we are going to be having a child together, we should at least try to be friends,' he added.

She heard his logic, understood it, but her heart, soul and body didn't want to be friends with Jago. Friends meant that he wouldn't stroke his big hands over her bare skin, drop kisses on her lips, skim his mouth across her stomach, down the inside of her legs.

'Say yes, Dodi. Don't make me go alone.'

'I'm pretty sure that you have at least fifteen women you can call up right now who would be happy to be your date.'

'Sure. But you're so much more interesting,' Jago said, his deep voice raising goosebumps on her skin.

Interesting, Dodi thought as he swung down her road and approached her boom gate. Was interesting a good or bad thing?

She didn't know and she wished she did.

CHAPTER EIGHT

JAGO PULLED UP in front of Dodi's double garage door, cut the engine to his car and raised his hand off the wheel, puzzled to see it trembling. Why?

He couldn't be nervous. He didn't get nervous. Scared? No!

Excitement, he eventually decided after picking up and discarding other emotions. He was excited to pick up a woman, to go on a date.

No, that was wrong. He was excited to see *Dodi*. To spend some time with her.

He hadn't seen her for ten days, but his mind often wandered in her direction, and he frequently had to resist the urge to check in with her, to see what she was up to, to see how she was doing, to make sure she was feeling okay. At the end of the day, it took everything he had not to head over to the salon or her house so that he could look into her smoky eyes, count the freckles on her nose, feel her luscious mouth under his.

And his nights were pure torture. He took a long time to fall asleep, and when he did he had X-rated dreams with Dodi in a starring role. This wasn't like him. He didn't get excited over a woman, didn't let anyone upset his equilibrium. He *never* allowed them to distract him from his work.

But Dodi frequently strolled into his mind during business meetings, plopped down and made him lose his train of thought. And when he wasn't trying to work out how she got him to talk about his dad and the past—subjects he never discussed—he still scanned the horizon for Dodi-related trouble. What could go wrong with her pregnancy, her business, *them*? And after the child was born, what then? How were they going to raise a kid together, how might they disagree, what were the potential obstacles and how could he solve them now...?

He'd never spent this much time thinking about a woman, ever. He should nip his little Dodi obsession in the bud before it got out of control.

He refused to fall under her spell and be at the mercy of any sex-, lust- or attraction-induced craziness. He'd seen how his parents had acted—hot, cold, on, off, up, down—and he liked stability, things to be even keel, no drama.

That was why he'd married Anju, remember?

And really, he had so many other things in his life demanding his attention. Micah and an employee from the events planning company they owned—a business his father had acquired for Liyana to run years ago, and which hadn't held her interest for long—had yet to find another venue for Thadie's wedding and they were rapidly running out of time.

Thadie had more online threats than usual and the attention from the media and general public had ramped up exponentially, so much so that Thadie had employed a bodyguard from the local arm of an international company specialising in personal protection.

Her stalker/harasser had managed to cancel the wedding venue and tried the same scam on the caterer and Thadie's florist. Luckily, they both called for confirmation, so those disasters were averted.

Thadie, and by extension he and Micah—and Dodi, he supposed—were all living on tenterhooks, waiting for the next axe to fall. And, honestly, his sister was looking like anything but the radiant bride. She was thinner than she'd been since she was a teenager, her face looked gaunt and her eyes haunted.

Thadie, her wedding, and his inconvenient attraction towards Dodi all took up a lot of mental energy, so much so that he hadn't spent a lot of time thinking about the fact that he was going to be a father, that Dodi was carrying his child. Or maybe he'd deliberately avoided thinking about his being a father because the idea scared him stupid.

He liked Thadie's twins, he really did, but he had no experience with kids and had never planned to have any—that was a very deliberate choice he had made early on. He was far too much like his dad. Theo had been more of a business coach and hard taskmaster-motivator than a hands-on father. He didn't know what a good dad looked like. He was abrupt and terse, impatient and competitive. What if he was as bad a father as his own had been?

Worse?

What if he failed at this most important of tasks? What then? Could he live with himself? He didn't think so. But neither could he walk away from his child, from Dodi—that wasn't an option! So here he sat, in no man's land.

Jago scrubbed his face with his hands and pushed his hand through his hair, before rubbing the back of his neck to ease the tension in his neck. He could either, he decided, sit in his car overthinking and over-analysing or he could get out, ring Dodi's doorbell and take an exceptionally attractive woman out to a charity event at a lovely venue in the heart of the city.

Leaving his suit jacket in the car, Jago walked up the path to Dodi's front door and rang the doorbell. He heard her shout telling him she was coming and a few minutes later she yanked the door open, dressed only in a short, silky nightrobe clinging to her damp body.

Jago's eyes skimmed her body. She was not wearing anything under the thin fabric and immediately felt aroused. He swallowed and shoved down the urge to yank her into his arms, kiss her senseless and drop that gown to the hallway floor.

'God, I'm so late! I'm so sorry!' Dodi told him, pulling him inside the hall and slamming the door closed behind him. Her messy hair was piled up on her head, water ran down her skin into the vee at the bottom of her throat and her dark copper eyelashes were beaded with droplets. She'd literally just stepped out of the shower.

'Can you give me fifteen minutes…twenty?' Dodi gabbled.

Discombobulated, Jago stared at her profile, fighting the urge to kiss her. Then Dodi yawned and Jago noticed her pale complexion, the puffiness of her red eyes, her trembling lower lip. All thoughts of taking her to bed fled—well, okay, receded—and he placed a hand on her shoulder to halt her progress up the stairs. He turned her to face him and lifted her chin when she wouldn't meet his eyes.

'Hey, what's wrong? You look like you've been crying.'

Dodi nibbled on her bottom lip before shrugging. 'It's been a stunningly difficult day.'

Yeah, he could see that. It was in her dark, sad eyes, in the way the skin pulled across her high cheekbones, in her wobbly lip and chin. 'Workwise or pregnancy-wise?'

'Both. I've started with morning sickness, but my body seems to think it's something I should do a few times a day. And God, I'm tired. I've never known tiredness like this, ever.'

If she lived with him, he would've known about this. He could've called a doctor, made sure she got to bed early, helped her, dammit! Not wanting to start a fight, he swallowed down his irritation. 'Is that normal?'

Dodi shrugged. 'Apparently so. It hits some women harder than others.' She pulled a face. 'Lucky me.'

Dodi moved away from him to continue her dash up the stairs, but Jago stepped in front of her. 'Wait, what happened at work?'

Dodi closed her eyes and shrugged. 'Bad brides, horrible brides, demanding mothers, whiny bridesmaids.' She patted his chest. 'If I don't go on up, we are going to be late. Very late.'

He didn't care. 'They'll survive.' He was lucky enough to have carte blanche entry into all the best parties and events in the city, in most cities, and nobody would complain if he was late. The fundraisers knew that the presence of any Le Roux attending a charity event was a stamp of approval and he could walk in at any time he liked and they would welcome him with open arms.

It was the power his surname commanded.

Dodi swayed on her feet and Jago grabbed her by the hips to steady her. If anything, she looked paler than she had a few minutes before. 'When last did you eat, Elodie Kate?'

She scrunched up her nose, trying to think. 'Breakfast? An apple midmorning?'

He ground his teeth together. Not good enough. And he couldn't take her out until she felt a bit steadier on her feet, with a bit more colour in her cheeks. She needed food, stat.

And maybe an early night.

'Go on up, pull on something comfortable and I'll call Jabu and get him to bring us some food.'

She looked at him as if he'd grown an extra eye. 'You will not! Your butler doesn't need to cook me a meal and then drive forty minutes across town to deliver it.'

'There are at least a dozen meals he can whip up in a heartbeat. He loves to drive, and more than that, he loves to be useful. If I call him now, we can eat in about ninety minutes.'

Dodi shook her head, looking bemused. 'You could just order a takeout.'

'With no nutritional value? I don't think so.'

She looked at him, bemused but wide-eyed and lovely. 'What about your charity event?'

'I'll write them a bigger than expected cheque to compensate for my non-attendance.'

Dodi's eyes slammed into his and a small smile touched her lovely mouth. 'You keep surprising me, Jago.'

He was so tempted to pull her into his arms, to lower his mouth to hers. Not only because he wanted her—and he always wanted her—but because he wanted to give her a little comfort, some tenderness. And that was strange, weird, because tenderness wasn't something he was familiar with. Soft emotions made him feel vulnerable and uncomfortable and he tended to avoid them as much as possible.

Yet, around Dodi, they kept welling to the surface. And, for the first time ever, he didn't mind too much. The feelings he'd avoided for so long—vulnerability, tenderness, a hatred of being out of control—weren't quite as frightening with her as they'd been before.

Jago watched Dodi walk up the stairs, slower than normal, holding onto the bannister. He couldn't ask her to go out with him tonight. He could see that she was at the end of her tether, emotionally and physically. He couldn't expect her to do her hair, put on some make-up and be charming.

And he was more than okay with spending the evening in her colourful, slightly bohemian house, inhaling the calming scents of roses, perfume and beeswax, and the warm Highveld wind blowing in from the open doors leading to her courtyard. He was used to the best money could buy, beautifully designed furniture and eye-catching art, *space*, but he had no problem with sitting down on her bright red sofa and putting his bare feet on her coffee table, sipping on a beer as he watched a rugby match on TV. Or listening to music.

Or just talking to the woman carrying his baby.

Jago made his call to Jabu and pulled off his tie, dropping it onto the hall table, along with his phone, keys and wallet. After rolling up his sleeves, he walked into Dodi's kitchen and found a nearly full bottle of white wine in her fridge. He found a wine glass and poured himself a healthy measure.

He felt at home here in her quiet, fragrant house, he realised as he sipped his wine. He could hear Dodi moving around upstairs, the murmur of the turned-down stereo, the distant sound of a dog barking.

It felt normal and natural. He liked it.

He liked it a *lot*.

Dodi made the mistake of lying back on her bed, where she promptly fell asleep. She woke up to the sound of voices downstairs and low male laughter. Then her front door closed, and she heard a car starting up and accelerating away. Jago's butler had come and gone…

How long had she been upstairs?

Dodi, dressed in black three-quarter leggings and an oversize off-the-shoulder slouchy top the colour of oatmeal, pulled her hair up into a high, messy ponytail and headed downstairs. She placed her hand on the door frame to her kitchen and looked at Jago, who was standing at the island in the centre of the room, on which sat two ornate silver cloches.

'I fell asleep.' Dodi grimaced, walking over to the island. 'Again.'

Jago smiled at her. 'I know. I was worried about you, so I went up and saw you passed out on your bed.'

She looked at the clock on the wall and saw that nearly two hours had passed. 'What have you been doing with yourself?'

'I grabbed my laptop from my car and did some work,' Jago explained.

Dodi winced at her lack of hospitality. 'I'm so sorry.'

'You needed sleep—and I'm a big boy. I can look after myself.'

When it came to Jago Le Roux people thought him abrupt and cold, terse and tense, but under the designer suits he was nothing like that, Dodi decided. Six weeks ago, she'd thought him to be unemotional and a little robotic. Hot but austere. She now believed that his impassive facade hid a deeply feeling and sensitive man.

Jago had hidden Mariana-Trench-deep depths and she, damn her, wanted to dive. Dodi folded her arms across her chest and pinched the inside of her left arm, reminding herself that that way madness lay.

It would be so easy to fall for Jago, she thought, to allow herself to be swept away in the fantasy of falling in love with her baby's father. He was outrageously sexy, a fantastic lover, wealthy as Croesus and more thoughtful than she gave him credit for. But Dodi knew, better than most, that good things didn't last. She'd never felt secure with her parents, and she'd spent the bulk of her childhood and teens constantly worried whether one or the other parent would permanently abandon her, and which adult she'd be left with.

Lily's taking her in had been an offer from heaven and she'd only had eight years with her grandmother before she died, eight short years of being loved and adored before she was ripped away from her.

Dan, before they became lovers, had been her best friend since she was sixteen, her lover since she was eighteen, but he'd lied to her, constantly and consistently about so much over a long period. Along with cheating on her, he'd also sabotaged her friendships to ensure that she remained emotionally reliant on him. Had his lover not brought matters to the head, she might, by now, be married to him, not knowing he was manipulative and untrustworthy.

She adored and trusted Thadie but the only person she could fully count on was herself.

Dodi felt the headache building up behind her eyes and pushed her fingers into her temple, feeling a little lightheaded. A heartbeat later, Jago's arm encircled her waist and with no effort at all, and using only one arm, he lifted her off her feet and walked her over to the small, two-seater dining table tucked up against the wall and deposited her into a chair.

Stepping back, and efficient as always, he poured her a glass of ginger beer and pushed it into her hand. 'Drink that,' he ordered in a brusque voice.

Dodi sipped, felt the bubbles in her nose and sighed when the tart liquid slid down her dry throat. In a few minutes, the sugar would hit her system and she'd perk up. Maybe even enough to go to Jago's charity event.

Jago slid a small plate of crackers adorned with

finely sliced tomatoes, grated cheese and chives in front of her. 'I made these earlier because I was starving. Get some food into you, Dodi,' he gruffly told her. 'You look like a puff of wind could blow you away.'

Fair assessment. Dodi picked up a cracker, popped it into her mouth and chewed. She'd eat one, two if Jago gave her the beady eye, but probably no more. Food, generally, held no appeal.

Then the tart, slightly spicy mayonnaise hit her tongue and she moaned in pleasure, closing her eyes at the flavour bomb on her tongue. Swallowing, she picked up another cracker and demolished that. Soon, most of the crackers on the plate were gone and she felt, almost, like herself.

Jago flashed his devastating half-smile. 'Enjoyed that?'

She nodded and picked a crumb off her plate with the tip of her finger. 'They were delicious.'

He shrugged. He pointed to the cloches which still sat on the island. 'Are you ready for dinner or can you wait?'

Dodi lifted her feet to place her heels on the edge of her chair. She wouldn't be able to sit like this in a few weeks or months. 'I can wait.'

Jago refreshed her glass with ginger beer, added some mint picked from the small bush growing on her windowsill and finally some ice. After refilling his wine glass, he joined her at the table, resting his back against the wall and stretching out his long legs. 'Tell me about your horrible day.'

Dodi grimaced and shook her head. 'It's over. I'd rather move on.'

'Tell me, I want to know.'

Dodi ran her finger up and down her glass, breaking up the droplets of condensation. What to say? How to start? It had been a disaster of epic proportions. 'Saturdays are busy days at the salon but today was insane. We were slammed from the moment we opened, with both walk-ins and brides with appointments.

'Two of my consultants didn't arrive—they both sent me messages telling me that they had stomach flu.' She felt the same familiar spurt of annoyance she had earlier. 'But, since they are best friends and both previously asked me for the weekend off, I think them having stomach flu was a lie.'

Jago didn't suggest that she fire her staff members or discipline them, which she appreciated.

'Anyway, we were slammed, and I think the heat and the crowded salon started to work on everyone's nerves, from the staff to the brides to the brides' entourages. As the day went on, everybody started getting rattier and things started going wrong.'

'Like?' Jago asked when she stopped talking.

'Ah...well, a bride picked up five kilograms and couldn't fit into her very fitted dress. She blamed my most experienced dressmaker for taking the wrong measurements. A bride and her bridesmaid got into a heated argument when the bride chose a hideous colour and style for their dresses, and they ended up screaming at each other.'

Jago turned to face her, placing his bent forearms on the table, looking sexy and interested and...hot.

Concentrate, Dodi.

'Another bride insisted on a dress that was three

times her father's budget and he tried to pay for it using three different credit cards and all of them were declined. She flounced off in tears and he wasn't far off.'

Jago moved his hand so that he could run his finger on the inside of her wrist. It was, she was sure, a gesture of comfort, but it sent sparkles of desire rushing up her arm.

'It was a mess, all around. At one point I went into my office, put a pillow over my face and screamed at the top of my lungs.' And cried.

'Tough, tough day.'

It had been, Dodi agreed. But she'd made it through without killing or maiming anyone, so that had to be a win. So she just needed to keep doing that for the next, oh, thirty years or so.

'Can you hire someone to help you?' He closed one eye and grimaced. 'Can *I* hire someone to help you?'

She rolled her eyes at his suggestion. 'You cannot. And I don't need physical help, not really. Sometimes I'd just like to step away from the responsibility of it all.'

She could see the understanding in his eyes. Jago's responsibility wasn't to thirty people but to many thousands. God, how did he sleep? Jago sipped from his wine glass, and when he lowered it he looked thoughtful. 'Tell me the real reason you don't like the wedding dress business.'

Because it was a question she hadn't expected, it felt like he'd rammed a probe up her spine, sending two thousand volts of electricity through her body. Nobody but Jago suspected her of having a dislike-hate relationship with Love & Enchantment, knew that she dragged her butt to work every day. She'd adored her grandmother and knew how much she loved the salon, and the thought of anyone knowing how much she hated pouring brides into white-after-white-after-cream dresses made her feel sick to her stomach.

Lily had saved her from a dead-end life, given her a profitable business, a house, security, and telling anyone how she felt, really felt about the salon, made her feel intensely disloyal.

She sucked in a deep breath, prepared her lie. 'I just had a bad day, Jago, nothing more.'

He cocked his head to the side and touched the tip of his finger to the side of his nose. 'You always scrunch your nose up, just on the one side, when you lie.'

She did not! Did she?

'But I'm not lying,' she stated, forcing herself to look him in the eye. 'Bad day, annoying people. Let's move on.'

Jago dared to smile. 'Let's not. What's your problem with the business, Elodie Kate? And what would you be doing if you weren't a bridal salon owner?'

Oh, God, that was easy to answer. She might hate wedding dresses, but she loved fashion and she'd open a vintage clothing shop and decor shop. She could just see it, full of mid-century Swedish furniture and Italian lighting, Art Deco glass and great clothes from fantastic designers.

She sighed, reminding herself that she had a shop, one that she'd been given by a woman who loved her, who'd rescued her. Who'd expected her to carry on her legacy.

Dodi dropped her feet and faced him, placing one elbow on the table and resting her temple in the palm of her hand. She wanted to tell him, she realised. She wanted to unburden herself, to share the messy feelings of gratitude and resentment and discontent, hoping that he would understand.

'You're right, I have issues with the salon,' she quietly told Jago and immediately wished she could pull the words back. Because she felt colder now, swamped with an icy blanket of guilt and ingratitude.

Jago didn't look surprised. He slowly nodded. 'I've known that for a while. At Thadie's dress fitting, you were all business, totally in your head and on a mission to make sure the dresses were perfect. You seemed almost unmoved.'

Dodi grimaced. 'Dammit, I hope Thadie didn't realise that.'

'Nah, it was because I was watching you so closely that I noticed.'

'Why were you watching me so closely?' Dodi asked, confused.

Jago sent her a soft, heat-filled smile. 'Because I had brushed up against you earlier and I was transported back to that kiss. I was not only fighting my impulse to drag you into my arms but also trying to work out how my sister's best friend morphed into an even more stunning woman than the one I kissed five years ago. And why you did strange things to my blood pressure.'

His voice was like hot chocolate after playing in

the snow, tart lemonade after swimming in the sea. Soothing and rather wonderful. And he'd felt all of that? Really? 'Ah… I don't know what to say to that.'

But damn, I could kiss you. I could kiss you for the longest, longest time.

Jago cleared his throat, stood up and picked up his glass. He yanked the wine bottle out of the fridge and filled his glass before briefly resting the cold bottle against his forehead. He released a deep, loud sigh before replacing the bottle in the fridge. But instead of returning to his chair opposite her, he leaned against the island, crossing his ankles.

How she'd love to see him in jeans and a T-shirt, wearing board shorts…barefoot and bare-chested. He had a clotheshorse body and looked good in anything, even a pair of smart black trousers and a white shirt, but man, she'd love to see him in something different.

Naked. Naked would be good.

'Why do you hate working at Love & Enchantment, Dodi?'

Damn, they were back to this. Dodi wanted to deflect the question, tried to think of a subject change but couldn't raise the energy. And really, did it matter if Jago knew? He was the one person in the world who never blabbed—hell, he was so far from being a Chatty Kathy it wasn't even funny, and she knew he'd never share her secret and her shame.

'I feel like a fraud.' There, she'd said it.

Jago frowned, instantly puzzled. 'A fraud? Why?'

Dodi dragged her finger across the table, drawing imaginary pictures in her head. She couldn't look at him. If she did, she'd never get the words out.

'My grandparents had a fairy-tale relationship. By all accounts they were soul mates. My grandfather died when my father was young. Lily already had the bridal shop and she adored helping brides, loved hearing their 'meet-cute' stories and hearing about their fiancés and their weddings. She was so into love and weddings and happily-ever-afters. I used to tease her, tell her that she lived in a romance novel, that the real world didn't work like that,' Dodi said, smiling at the memories of her gran's outrage. 'She told me that one day I would fall in love, and I'd see what she was talking about.'

'I take it that didn't happen? Or maybe it did, and your relationship went sour?'

She wished she had such an easy explanation. 'Not exactly.' Dodi tapped her finger against the table, the sound of her nail hitting the wood filling the silence. 'To explain, I need to tell you about my parents. My father was Lily's only child, and he was…different. Difficult. Fantastically intelligent but impulsive and free-spirited and stubborn. He met my mum at university. Met? No, that's too tame a word. I sensed that they collided, smashed into each other. Two wilful, spoiled, sexual creatures who wanted what they wanted when they wanted it.'

She stopped, feeling like a cork about to shoot out of its bottle. She'd never spoken to anyone about her parents and how she felt about them.

'Get it out, Elodie Kate.'

'I was an afterthought, something or someone they were burdened with. A drag.' Dodi felt a cold hand clutch her heart, and she was a child again, feeling helplessness and bone-deep fear. 'They hated being lumbered with me and didn't bother to hide their frustration from me.

'They wanted to be free, to circle each other, to move away, to come back, but I was the unwanted heirloom they didn't want and couldn't get rid of. Neither of them wanted me permanently. They took turns leaving, both married and divorced other people, remarried each other, divorced, and their biggest arguments were over me and who had custody of me. I was never sure where I would live, on whose doorstep I'd land, whether I'd like my new stepmother or stepfather.'

'Jesus, Dodi.'

'My father cut off all communication with my grandmother around the time my parents married, and Lily lost track of them. She wasn't even aware she had a granddaughter until I landed on her doorstep.'

He frowned. 'I don't understand.'

Why would he? 'Shortly before my sixteenth birthday, my parents concocted a plan. They were done with me, that much they agreed on. My dad told me to pack a bag, that we were taking a trip. We landed at Lily's, he told her I was his granddaughter and that he was going out for a while, to give us time to become acquainted. He didn't return, didn't answer our calls, and two days later the rest of my stuff arrived by courier.'

As she'd expected, Jago looked horrified. 'That's… diabolical,' he stated, anger in his voice.

'I later learned that Lily was as caught off guard as I was but, God bless her, she rallied and she let me stay,' Dodi explained. 'Living with her was like entering an alternative reality. I had chores and curfews and had to go to school every day and bring home decent reports. I had to do an extramural activity and some sort of exercise, eat healthily.'

'And you rebelled?'

She grinned. 'On the contrary, I loved every rule, every regulation. I'd had none, so I loved the rules, knowing what I could and could not do. And Lily's rules made me feel secure, loved, cared for. Can you understand that?'

Jago rubbed his jaw. 'I guess. So, you were happy with your gran?'

'Happier than I'd ever been in my life. I met Dan, at uni I met Thadie, and my life was truly excellent, you know?'

'Who is Dan?'

No, she couldn't talk about him, not yet. Maybe not ever. She waved his question away. 'I was so happy with Lily and we were close. We often spoke about my parents and the shop. She told me I was too young to be so cynical about love and marriage, I told her she was living in La-La Land. She told me I would change my mind at some point.'

'But you haven't.'

She shook her head. No, thanks to Dan, she was even further away than she was before. 'Sometimes I look at those starry-eyed brides and I want to shake them and tell them that a gorgeous dress and a stunning wedding means nothing, and that it won't always lead to sunshine and roses.'

Jago's intense eyes were laser-like on her face. 'Do

you not think they realise that? That they just want the experience of their union being celebrated before they settle down to the hard work of marriage?'

Dodi jerked her shoulders up to her ears. 'I don't know. Did Anju feel like that? Was your marriage hard work?' she asked, curious.

The skin tightened across his face and his lips thinned. 'I wasn't in love with Anju, and she didn't love me. We didn't have a white, church wedding. Our marriage was a marriage, I suppose, of convenience. Both of us were very clear about what we wanted from each other.'

Wow.

'And that was?' Would he answer? She wasn't sure.

'A meeting of minds. We were very good friends who shared a lot of the same interests. Good sex…we were very compatible in bed. Neither of us wanted children and we were both focused on our careers. She was unemotional, as am I. Our lives were a drama-free zone and that was important to me.'

'And it worked for you?'

'Yeah, it did. Maybe we weren't happy, but we were content.'

He dropped his head to look into his half-empty wine glass, idly swishing the liquid around inside. He opened his mouth to speak, then shook his head. 'I think that's enough for now, Dodi. Maybe we should eat.'

She wasn't hungry…well, not for food anyway. And yes, maybe they should stop talking because he was fascinating mentally *and* emotionally. She couldn't afford to start having feelings for him, to fall in love with him, to be anything but his friend and the woman who was carrying his child. Too many people had smacked her heart around, and she would not allow Jago Le Roux the same opportunity.

No, she wouldn't allow herself to think like that, to let thoughts of fascination and fondness settle in her mind. She was attracted to Jago, that was all that was happening here. She was conflating sex with emotions, and that was a very dangerous thing to do.

She had to separate the two, now…*immediately.*

To remind herself that she was in control, that she knew what she was doing—that she knew the difference between sex and love—Dodi approached him and placed her flat hand above his heart, her other hand sliding up his chest to curl around his neck. She wanted the crackle and the fizz, to be hit by lust and passion. And if feeling like that pulled her out of her bleak mood and from reliving her tiresome day, then she considered that a bonus.

'Will you kiss me, Jago?' she murmured, looking at him from under her lashes.

He put his hands behind him and gripped the edge of the island's granite top, holding on tight, as if he was forcing himself to stop himself from reaching for her. 'I don't know if I'll be able to stop myself from doing more,' Jago admitted.

Dodi rested her forehead on his sternum, inhaling his fresh, clean scent. 'I'd like you to take me away from today. Take me out of my head and take me to bed, Jago. Please?'

She'd beg if she had to, she needed him that much. Needed his confident and clever hands, his deep voice painting words on her skin, his mouth trailing fire over her body. The perfection of him sliding inside her, the intense explosion he pulled up inside her.

She needed the distraction, but more than that, she needed him.

The thought scared her, but when he bent his legs and carried her over to her sofa, it didn't scare her enough to resist.

CHAPTER NINE

MAN, HE WAS LUCKY.

Lucky to be here, having Dodi look at him with fire in her eyes, want chasing need across her face. He couldn't wait to get his hands on her, to cover her body with his, to slide into her. But between now and then, there was a wonderland to explore. And Lord, what a place it was.

He loved every single freckle, perfectly imperfect dots on her pale skin, he thought as he gently pulled her top up and over her head, revealing her pretty mint-green lacy bra. Through the lace, he could see the outline of her nipples and he had to restrain himself from pulling her bra cup aside and taking her in his mouth.

This evening he wanted slow and sexy. To discover and to delight.

Her eyes met his and he lost himself in all that blue, smoky and intense. His breath caught in his throat, his heart-rate increased and he forced himself to look away, uncomfortable with the emotion bubbling away in his chest. This was sex, he reminded himself. A physical connection between two people who were attracted to each other…

Then why did it feel like something so much more? Something deeper, darker, intense?

Dodi curled her hand around his neck and pulled his head down to hers, a silent entreaty to kiss her. Soft lips, a spicy mouth, heat. Kissing wasn't something he usually enjoyed—it was usually a means to an end—but he could kiss Dodi for hours without needing a beginning or an end.

But soon his hands itched with impatience, and he moved his fingers to her lower back, down her fabric-covered butt. Her leggings had to go, so he gently pulled them down her hips and over her pretty feet, tipped in pale pink polish, dropping them to land on the floor next to the sofa. He felt Dodi's hands working his shirt buttons and, impatient with the delay, Jago reached behind his head to grab the back of his collar, pulling off the shirt in one movement, sighing when her hands stroked his chest, the ball of his shoulder.

They spent long, drugged-out moments kissing and touching, exploring, using their hands and mouths, teeth and tongues. It was sexy and seductive, a world of sensation. Jago placed his hand on her bare knee and slowly worked his way up her thigh, his fingers brushing the fabric between her legs. He knew she was damp and hot and, judging by the way she softly panted, in need of what he could give her. She lifted her hips and he pulled his hand away, wanting to delay her satisfaction, knowing he could take her higher and faster. He palmed her butt with his hand, kneading her, smiling when she released a little growl of frustration.

Using his other hand, Jago pulled her hairband loose and shoved his fingers into her heavy mass of hair, clasping her head and angling her face to receive his no-holds-barred kiss. Tongues danced as he devoured her mouth, learning her, tasting her, pushing her for more.

The last of her inhibitions left her and, encouraged by his passion and groans of appreciation, Dodi let her hands streak over his body, tracing the rows of his stomach and the long muscles covering his hips, brushing over his hard erection.

Such a brief touch but it sent reverberations up his spine, shooting pleasure into his brain. He must've said something, he knew not what, but she touched him more firmly, dragging her thumb along the length of his fabric-covered shaft.

'I love the way you touch me,' Jago muttered against her now bare breast, before sucking her nipple against the roof of his mouth. She arched her back, and fumbled for the clasp of his trousers, equally frustrated with the barriers between them.

Needing a minute to slow down, to lower his racing pulse, he looked down at her, his eyes skimming over her breasts, over her still flat stomach to her long legs. Those pretty feet.

'Perfect. You are so very lovely.'

'You're pretty hot yourself, Le Roux,' Dodi told him, sliding down the zip of his fly. 'But I think this would work better if we got rid of these.'

That made sense. Pulling away from her, Jago yanked off his shoes and socks and pushed his underwear and trousers down his hips in a quick, efficient slide. Stepping out of the fabric, he lay on his side next to Dodi, resting his hand on her stomach and sliding his mouth across her lips. He briefly thought about getting a condom—protection was a habit—remembered they didn't need one and smiled. He couldn't wait to make love to her with no barriers between them.

Jago slid his hand between her legs and cupped her, his thumb immediately finding and brushing her hot core through her thong, causing her to gasp, then sigh.

'That's so hot and I want more.' Dodi moaned the words. 'I need more… I need *you*.'

He tested her again, knew she was ready for him, dispensed with her panties and, with one hand under her hips, moved her under him so that she lay in the centre of the sofa. He wished he were in her bed—he needed space to move and briefly considered carrying her up the stairs but knew he couldn't wait, not a second more, to slide inside her and to make her his.

But he had to be careful, to take it slow. He was long and thick, and her taking him inside her meant she would have to accommodate and stretch and… man, she felt so amazingly good.

He'd never felt like this before, when being inside a woman felt like coming home, the best place to be.

On that thought, Jago hooked his big hands under her thighs and lifted her, spreading her legs so that he could fill her completely, as well as making contact with her ultra-sensitive clitoris.

Jago pinned her down with his body, pulling back and sliding into her again with one long, sure stroke. He felt himself dissolving from the inside out as his world narrowed to what was happening between them.

Everything faded away and there were only her hands on his butt, nails digging into his flesh, her tongue in his mouth as he kissed her endlessly, the upward thrust of her hips as she met him stroke for stroke.

She needed to come because he was fast losing control. 'I'm not going to be able to hang on,' Jago told her, his forehead against hers. He moved his head to talk in her ear. 'Take all of me, darling. Yeah…use me… Fly, dammit!'

'Harder…' Dodi told him, her body arching as she reached for her release.

Jago rocked into her, as hard as he dared, and she shouted as she clenched around him. Stars exploded behind his eyeballs, at the base of his spine, as his body splintered into a million pieces. He vaguely heard Dodi panting beneath him, knew that she'd lifted her arm to place it over her eyes, but he was in another dimension, someplace indescribably lovely.

Yet, for some reason, he knew this wasn't the end, not quite, so he moved his hips again and, still hard, touched something deep inside her. Dodi slammed her head back into the cushion, scrunched her eyes shut and screamed his name before she fractured again. He orgasmed again too, not so big and bold this time but still crazy good. Two orgasms, one massive…had that ever happened to him before?

He didn't think so.

Minutes, hours or years might have passed before they returned to reality, came back down to earth and Jago rolled off her and pulled so that she lay on top of him, her cheek resting above his heart, his arms cradling her close.

Dodi yawned and then he heard the unmistakable sound of her stomach rumbling. He laughed and patted her bottom. 'I need to get some food into you. You need your strength.'

She yawned and nodded. 'Mmm, I have to start eating better. This baby saps me of all my energy.'

'That's one reason. The other is that I intend on taking you upstairs and doing this, and more, again. Are you up for that?'

She lifted her head to look at him, her eyes soft and sweet. Then her smile turned wicked. 'Oh, I'm up for anything, Le Roux.'

The next morning, Dodi agreed to accompany Jago to an upscale farmers' market north of the city, where he was meeting his twin, and Thadie and her kids, for breakfast. It was family time, he explained, something they did every month or so.

Dodi knew of their monthly breakfast date and was honoured to be invited to join them. She just didn't know how she was going to explain why she was with Jago, how she was going to answer Thadie's curious questions.

She wasn't ready to tell Thadie that she was sleeping with her brother and was definitely not ready to tell her that she was carrying his baby. Partly because Thadie was stressed out of her mind and partly because she didn't know how her relationship with Jago—could it even be called a relationship?—would affect the most important relationship in her life.

She couldn't lose Thadie. It would kill her.

Walking alongside Thadie, who was dressed in

a short, pretty, lime-green sundress, enormous sunglasses and flat sandals, Dodi waited for the interrogation to start. Any minute now Thadie would ask her why she and Jago were together so early on a Sunday morning.

I was in the shower with him just a couple of hours ago and he had his hands…

No, she couldn't tell her that. There were some things her best friend didn't need to know, especially when it came to her older brother.

Thadie stopped to look at leather handbags and Dodi looked around, her eyes immediately going to Jago's broad back. They'd briefly stopped at his house so that he could change into a loose, linen shirt and tan cargo pants. He wore expensive leather flips-flops on his feet and a pair of dark sunglasses covered his eyes. Micah wore board shorts and a green T-shirt, and he was pushing the double pram holding the chattering twins, who were dressed in cute matching outfits of denim shorts and patterned T-shirts.

Thadie's bodyguard hovered a few steps behind her, dressed casually but on high alert.

'I need coffee,' Thadie declared, gesturing to a stall selling upmarket coffee. 'Do you want a cup?'

Dodi just managed to stop herself from shuddering. The smell of coffee made her want to hurl. 'I think I'll have fruit juice instead.'

Knowing that Thadie would ask her what was wrong with her—up until she'd fallen pregnant, coffee was her favourite food group—Dodi attempted to distract her. 'Where's Clyde?'

Thadie pulled her towards the cart selling coffee. 'He plays golf every Sunday.'

Dodi didn't think the world would stop turning if Clyde skipped golf once in a while.

'Besides, I told him I needed to spend some time with my brothers before the wedding, as a family. I haven't seen much of them, or you, lately. It's *so* nice to see you.'

Dodi pushed her hand into the crook of Thadie's elbow. 'I know, I'm so sorry. It's been mad. Are you okay?'

Thadie joined the line for coffee and stared down at the dusty floor, her shoulders lifting. 'I don't know. I'm getting married in a month and it's starting to get real, you know?'

A bit too real? Real enough and scary enough for her to call it off? She was debating whether she should verbalise her concerns about Thadie's marriage when she saw a very familiar person, walking hand in hand with a dark-haired woman. She sucked in her breath, feeling a little lightheaded.

She'd hadn't seen him since the day she broke up with him, a couple of days after Lily's death and before her funeral, and Dan looked just the way she remembered him, with his thick hair and his glasses falling halfway down his nose. He was dressed in his usual summer uniform of shorts and a boldly patterned printed shirt, this one in bright yellows and greens.

As if feeling her eyes on him, Dan looked around and he jerked, just a little, when he recognised her.

He lifted his hand, sort of waved and sent a swift smile. God, Johannesburg had a population of six million people and she had to run into Dan at a farmers' market outside of the city. What were the chances and why was life punishing her like this?

Dan mouthed some words and she wished she could pretend that she couldn't understand him. *Are you okay?*

No, I'm not okay, she wanted to scream. *You cheated on and lied to me, played mind games with me!*

Dodi closed her eyes and shook her head, instinctively wrapping her hands around her middle, feeling as if she was about to fall apart. Losing his friendship, that closeness, still made her heart ache, dammit.

When she opened her eyes, she saw a woman tugging him away. He looked back, just once, his face filled with sadness and regret. But Dodi knew he wasn't sorry. He'd loved making her life hell. Dan was an excellent actor.

'Dan doesn't look a day older,' Thadie commented.

She nodded, unable to speak.

Thadie rubbed her upper arm, giving her comfort. 'Still hurts, huh?'

'I think it always will,' Dodi reluctantly admitted. She wished she could forget about him, forgive him for what he'd done, but she couldn't. He'd played with her mind, her life and her emotions, and betrayed their friendship.

She'd never allow anyone to do that to her again. She'd never give anyone that amount of emotional power over her again.

Dodi glanced over to Jago and saw that he was standing a little way from them, talking to the bodyguard and Micah. The three men, tall, fit and devastatingly good-looking, were garnering a lot of attention, mostly female. There was a lot of hair-twirling, flirty smiles, looks over shoulders. None of them noticed.

Dan was in the past, and she had a baby to focus on, so Dodi pushed back her shoulders and decided to forget about her waste-of-oxygen ex and enjoy the time with her best friend.

Thadie pulled her glasses off her face, folded the arms and tapped them against her palm. 'So, did you hear that Jago has rented out his house?'

It was a blatant change of subject but one that made Dodi's mouth drop open in shock. Hadleigh House? His family home? 'But that house has been in your family for decades! Where are he and Micah going to live? What about the staff?'

Thadie rolled her eyes. 'Not Hadleigh, goose! His own house, the one he lived in with Anju.'

Oh! *That* house. Dodi raised her eyebrows. 'Really?'

'Mmm. He sent in the movers, and they packed everything up. He asked me where he could donate her clothes, sent her books to a second-hand shop, sent other stuff to her family. He took a couple of days off work last week to sort through the house.'

Really? *Wow.*

'My oldest brother is different,' Thadie commented after a short silence. 'More relaxed, warmer. Would you know why?'

Oh, God, the interrogation was about to start. Dodi placed her hand on her heart, forcing her eyes wide. 'Why would I know?'

Thadie narrowed her eyes at her. 'You suck at lying, Do. What is going on with you two?'

Dodi was about to reply when Jago's familiar scent

hit her nose and his hand landed on her lower back. 'The boys want to visit the mini petting zoo, so Micah and I thought we'd head over there. It'll give you two a little time alone,' he said.

She scowled at him. Honestly, this wasn't the time for him to be considerate! Dodi widened her eyes in panic, desperately hoping Jago would read her mind and suggest something they could all do together. Anything to prevent the cross-examination she was bound to face if she and Thadie were left alone.

Thadie sent her a wicked grin. 'What a wonderful idea! Dodi and I have so much to catch up on and we'd love a little girl time!'

Dodi grimaced. Thadie was her best friend and she loved her, but knew how relentless she could be when she knew something was afoot. Dodi looked at the broad backs of the departing Le Roux brothers and wished she were going with them. Dragging her feet, she followed Thadie to a table under a white tent and knew that within ten minutes Thadie would know that a) Dodi was sleeping with her brother, and b) she was going to be their baby's aunt.

She and Jago wanted to keep the news to themselves for a bit longer, but that wasn't going to happen because there was no way she was going to lie to her best friend. Oh, well, Dodi thought, shrugging.

It was all Jago's fault for being kind and thoughtful. As they said, no good deed went unpunished.

'I cannot believe you didn't tell me earlier! How could you keep this from me?' Thadie demanded via a video call, later that evening.

They'd covered this ground earlier when Dodi finally admitted that she was pregnant and that Jago was the father of her baby.

'You have a lot on your plate, Thads, and I didn't want to take attention away from you and your wedding,' Dodi explained, *again.*

Thadie waved her words away. 'My best friend is having my brother's baby! That's something I needed to know.'

'Sorry,' Dodi apologised. Again. For what felt like the hundredth time. But she knew Thadie was more excited than mad, and that there wasn't any heat behind her accusations.

'I hope you have a boy—I really do. But I also hope you have a girl…oh, a girl would be magical!' Thadie rattled on, her dark eyes dancing with joy. 'Maybe you'll have twins!'

Her heart lurched in fear. Two babies? No, thank you! 'Shut your mouth,' she told Thadie.

Thadie's laugh sounded a little wicked. 'Twins are exactly what you deserve for keeping this news from us.'

When Jago, Micah and the twins had rejoined them this morning at the market, Thadie immediately asked Jago whether he had something to tell Micah and Jago instantly knew the game was up. Their eyes had connected, she'd shrugged and, after scowling at Thadie, he told Micah that she was pregnant and that the baby was his.

Micah, to his credit, had simply raised his eyebrows, kissed her cheek and given Jago one of those half-hugs men excelled at.

Dodi had no doubt Jago had received a *What the hell?* phone call from his twin.

'So, I'm still not clear on something…'

Oh, God, she knew what was coming.

'Are you and Jago together or not?' Thadie demanded.

How could she answer that question when she had no idea what they were, nor how they were going to be?

The best way to answer Thadie was, Dodi quickly decided, to distract her. 'Your bridesmaids' dresses arrived. We need to arrange a final fitting.'

'Stop trying to change the subject! Are you and Jago—?'

Dodi slapped her hand to her mouth, faked a heave and waved her hands in the air. 'Got to go! Morning sickness!'

Thadie still managed to get a few words in as she fumbled to disconnect the call. 'You are such a liar, Elodie Kate Davis!'

She was. Absolutely.

Exhausted by the long day and Thadie's interrogations, she walked from Jago's private sitting room onto his balcony and saw that he was talking on his phone. Seeing her, he wrapped up his conversation.

'That was Micah, checking in.'

Dodi dropped into the sofa next to him, sighing at how comfortable it was. The space was protected from the elements but still, a sofa this expensive, this lovely, shouldn't be outside. Ever.

'Let me guess…he wants to know whether we are together or not.'

'Yep.'

Dodi narrowed her eyes. 'And I bet your nosy sister nagged him to call.'

'Yep.'

Dodi pulled a face. 'God, she's relentless.'

Jago stretched out his long legs, linking his hands on his stomach, his expression thoughtful. 'We're all determined people—having a father like Theo, it's inevitable. But Thadie got a double dose. It's the only trait she inherited from our father, thank God.'

'You didn't like him much, did you?' Dodi asked.

'Did you like him?' he countered.

'I hardly knew him,' she replied. 'But he was always charming to me.'

'Of course he was—that was how he was with most people,' Jago bitterly replied. 'That wasn't the person he was at his core.'

'So who was he, Jago?'

Jago ran his finger up and down the side of his cold beer bottle. 'Theo established Le Roux International himself. He didn't have any family money behind him. He hustled and lied, ducked and dived, made promises he couldn't keep, over-promised and under-delivered. But somehow, because he was so damn charismatic, he made it work. Even when the business took off, even after he made his first million, billion, he still couldn't stick to the truth. Sometimes I think he lied to keep people unbalanced, because it was fun, to see if he could get away with it, and he always did. He was Theo Le Roux, wealthy, successful, with this huge personality and he was feted and adored.'

Dodi heard the bitter tone in his voice. 'Did he lie to you? To your siblings?'

Jago's expression tightened. 'All the time. He made promises to us, and my mum, that he never kept. He said we could get a dog one day, changed his mind the next. Said that if I got a B plus for maths I could get a motorbike, the next report card I needed to get an A, then when I did the goalposts moved again. He promised to join us on holiday, never did. Promised us he'd be there for Christmas, missed many of those.'

So much bitterness, so much pain.

'He treated my mum badly, kept her constantly off-balance, neurotic. Praising her one moment, belittling her the next. He did that to Micah and me as well. One day we were his favourite child, the next day we were scum on his shoe. He pitted us against each other, created competitions, fostered enmity. He hated that we were so close and tried whatever he could to come between us, between us and our mum. Everything was always about him, all the time.

'My father fed off drama and he loved arguments, fights, confrontation. His volatility was the reason I learned to read people and situations. I learned to anticipate trouble and how to take control of a situation, how to make it work for me, and, more importantly, my siblings. Because of him, I have back-up plans for my back-up plan.'

Dodi winced. She hadn't had the most functional of childhoods, it had been ridiculously unstable, but she hadn't lived in a war zone. Theo had been an emotional abuser, she realised. She wondered if Jago knew and accepted that.

Jago picked up his beer bottle and pointed it at her stomach. 'He's the reason I'm terrified of being a father. I'm scared I will do to my kid what my dad did to me.'

Dodi's mouth gaped open in shock. 'That's the most ridiculous thing I've ever heard!'

'Why? I am very like my father,' Jago replied, sounding super-reasonable. 'I'm demanding, competitive, married to my job. I'm impatient and abrupt.'

'You also love your brother and sister and treat them with kindness and respect. Sure, you're very straightforward, but you aren't cruel and you don't play mind games!' Dodi protested.

'How do you know, Dodi? You haven't spent that much time with me.'

How did she know? She wasn't sure, but she did. She'd somehow managed to pull away some of that hard shell and peek below the surface, and the man underneath the tough exterior was softer and more sensitive than the world realised. Someone who wanted a family, to love and be loved in return.

But he, like her, was too scared of taking that chance, of being hurt again.

'Who was the guy at the farmers' market today?'

Dodi blinked at his change of subject and flushed when his words sank in. 'Uh…who?'

Jago glared at her. 'Don't treat me like an idiot, Dodi. You and Thadie were both staring at him like he was a threat.'

Dammit! She'd hoped Jago hadn't noticed. A stupid wish because there was nobody more observant than the older Le Roux twin and she now knew why. It was because his father had made him that way.

'Dan? Well…uh…that's a long story.'

'I'm not going anywhere,' Jago told her.

Dammit.

CHAPTER TEN

ONLY THADIE KNEW the whole story, knew how Dan had blindsided and betrayed her. How much it hurt and that she felt like the world's biggest idiot for not having seen through him years ago. That thinking of him, what he'd done, was like taking a knife to her belly and slowly cutting herself open.

'Please tell me, Do.'

It was that soft 'please' that did it, the look in his eyes telling her she could trust him. But could she, though? She didn't know…

But Jago had been brave enough to tell her about his father and his childhood. Surely she could tell him about Dan's betrayal?

Where to start? When they'd met was as good a place as any. 'Lily sent me to a high school down the road from her house, a huge school with thousands of students. I'd only ever attended small, rural schools, so I was lost and scared and completely overwhelmed. Dan found me, scooped me up and took me under his wing. He wasn't the most popular guy around, but neither was he bullied…he was normal, I guess. He had a group of friends, guys and girls, and he pulled me into his group. I felt blessed and grateful to have a group.'

Jago's gaze was steady on her face. 'That sounds pretty normal.'

One would think. 'Yes, it does. Except that I'd make a new friend or be invited out on a date, and it would be fine for a week or two and then I'd be dropped like a hot potato. It happened a few times and I couldn't understand it because I didn't do anything wrong. Dan would hold me while I cried and tell me not to worry about them, that he and I were friends and nothing else mattered. It happened five, maybe six times, and I stopped going on dates, trying to make friends, because it hurt so much. Dan became my only friend, and he was my lifeline, my support structure, everything that mattered to me. We became lovers in my final year of school and remained together until just before my grandmother died.'

'So what happened that caused you to break up?'

Right, straight to the heart of the matter. 'A couple of weeks before Lily died, I was trying to nurse her, run her salon, and also trying to come to terms with her imminent passing. One day I got a call from a woman telling me that she and Dan had been having an affair for a few months.'

Jago winced. 'Ouch.'

'Yeah. Naturally, I didn't believe her, but she sent me pictures of them together, text messages, emails. Dan had told her that he didn't love me, couldn't stand me but he was worried I'd do something if he broke up with me. Some of the things he said about me were truly horrible.'

Jago said something indistinct but distinctly uncomplimentary about her ex and Dodi almost smiled.

She might as well tell him the rest, although it wasn't a pretty story. 'His lover, mistress, whatever, then told me something else that rocked my world.'

Jago's eyebrows rose, waiting for her to continue.

'So, back at school, those friends I made? Well, Dan bragged to her that he poisoned the well. As soon as he saw there was a connection, he went to them and quietly told them I was talking about them behind their backs, that I was playing with them, that I thought they were trash. He said that I was a little unbalanced and that they shouldn't confront me, that it might push me over the edge. Naturally, they dumped me, and I had no idea why.

'It kept happening, even at university—Dan and I went to the same one—and into my twenties, and I eventually stopped trying to make friends altogether. I didn't want to get hurt any more. I thought I was destined to have one friend, one lover.'

'But you and Thadie remained friends. He didn't manage to come between you.'

She shrugged. 'We shared a flat. He couldn't be there all the time. He and Thadie hated each other. She tried to tell me he was separating me from people, that he was trying to isolate me, but I didn't—couldn't, wouldn't—believe her.'

Jago grimaced.

'He saw me as *his*, his project, his property. He didn't particularly want me, hence the many flings and affairs, but he didn't want anyone else to have me either. If his lover hadn't called me, I would've married him,' Dodi admitted. 'It scares me to think that he would've manoeuvred me into marrying him.'

Dodi looked at Jago and tried, and failed, to smile. 'I have this thing about being pushed where I don't want to go, Jago.'

Would he hear her message, understand what she was trying to say?

Jago took a sip of his beer, looking thoughtful. 'Doesn't everyone want to make their own decisions, be in charge of their destiny?' he quietly asked.

'I'm sure they do.' Dodi leaned forward and captured her hands between her thighs. 'But it's a big thing for me because I've found myself in situations that I didn't choose, and they changed my life.'

'Being sent to live with your grandmother without warning, being cheated on, inheriting a business you didn't want,' he mused.

Exactly! 'I promised myself I wouldn't allow myself to ever be put in a situation that wasn't of my choice again.' She looked down at her hands and sighed. 'That's why this…this…thing with you is so hard. I didn't choose to have this baby—'

'I thought you said you wanted it,' Jago interjected, frowning.

Dodi waved her hands around, frustrated. 'I do! I'm just getting used to the idea and the fact that it's, once again, something that's been thrust on me.'

'And on me,' Jago pointed out.

Fair enough.

'I hear you, Elodie Kate. The thing is, we don't have to figure everything out right now. We have time.'

Seven months could, and would, fly past. They didn't have as much time as they thought.

The sound of Jago setting his beer bottle on the wrought-iron table disturbed the quiet, lazy summer evening. Here at Hadleigh House, she could pretend they weren't in the middle of a metropolis, living in a sprawling city. She felt as though she were on a country estate, far away from the hustle of city life. It was fast becoming her favourite place to be.

But this place wouldn't mean anything if Jago wasn't in it. It would be just another house filled with expensive stuff, but Jago made it home.

Home. Dear Lord...*home?* Or was home wherever Jago was, where she wanted to be? She thought it might just be because... Oh, *God.*

'Dodi?'

She blinked, trying to focus and his intense expression came back into focus. 'I am your baby's father and yes, while the thought of raising a child scares me, I do want to be part of the process. Don't doubt that, sweetheart. I'm not going anywhere.'

She saw the sincerity in his expression and the tenderness in his eyes. She was starting to trust him, she admitted silently. Panic coated her throat and lodged on her tongue. She loved being with him, sleeping with him, enjoyed their chats, but it would be stupid to trust him, or anyone else, with her very fragile heart.

She should tell him they couldn't go anywhere, that they'd run out of road. She wanted to suggest that they be lovers until they tired of each other...

She scoffed at her thoughts. She doubted she'd ever

tire of having Jago in her arms, in her body or her bed. Because…

Could she say it, even to herself? Could she even think it?

Was she, maybe, possibly, falling for Jago? Could she be falling in love with him?

Dodi stared at him, knowing she needed to try and talk herself out of the notion but knowing it was impossible. Some part of her—whether it was little or big was yet to be decided—was in love with Jago. God help her.

He couldn't know, not yet…possibly not ever. Would he hear it in her voice, see it in her eyes? She couldn't let that happen, not before she regained control, pushed it away.

She finally, finally, found the courage to meet his eyes and was surprised to see an understanding smile. 'It's overwhelming, right?' he softly asked. He was talking about the baby, thank God. He had to be.

'Very,' she admitted. She sighed, thinking that she could do with some time alone, to think.

Jago stood up and picked up his empty beer bottle. 'It's been a long day and we're both tired, played out.'

How did he do that? How did he know what she was feeling, what she needed without her having to say a word?

'Okay,' Dodi agreed, following him to his feet.

Jago walked around the table to where she stood and gently gripped her chin in his big hand and looked down into her face, his expression intense. 'You're going to have to trust someone at some time, Elodie Kate. I hope that person is me.'

She managed a small smile, a quick nod and tried not to sigh when Jago dropped a hard kiss on her open mouth. 'Come to bed now,' he softly suggested.

She stared at his broad hand for a moment before sliding her own hand into it and following him back into his sitting room, and then into his bedroom, wishing she could tell him that trust was an essential part of love, and if she couldn't trust him, she couldn't love him.

Wouldn't let herself love him.

Because loving, and losing, Jago would destroy her. There would be no climbing out if she toppled into that deep abyss.

Unable to sleep, Jago left Dodi in his bed, walked outside, and dived into the pool. After swimming for nearly an hour, and still feeling edgy, he sat on the side of the massive pool, his feet dangling. Water ran down his body, from his hair, and his limbs felt hot and heavy.

Normally exercise cleared his head, sharpened his thinking, but that hadn't happened tonight. If anything he was more confused than ever.

And it was all Dodi's fault.

The woman disoriented him, made him feel a hundred emotions at once, spun him in a thousand directions simultaneously.

Leaning back on his hands, Jago looked up at the bright moon, immediately seeing the rabbit shape on its surface, something one could only see from the southern hemisphere. He inhaled the fragrant air, heat mingling with the smell of roses from the extensive garden to his right. He smiled at the deep bellow of a bullfrog. Even in the city, he still felt connected to primal Africa. It was in her heat, her smells, her sounds and her essence. But saying that, he needed to get into the bush, somewhere wild, and he wanted to take Dodi with him.

Would Dodi agree to step away with him, to go to an unknown place with few roads, no mobile phone reception and no people? He wasn't sure. After hearing how her piece-of-crap ex had treated her, he finally understood Dodi's reluctance to trust, didn't blame her for being wary about people and men.

But he still wanted her to trust him, to know, deep down, that he would never, ever hurt her or their child. She needed to accept that she was under his protection and that he'd rather die than see her in any sort of distress.

Yes, he was protective of her, would be protective of his kid, but there was so much more to his feelings for his sister's best friend than his need to shield her.

He adored her body and loved being naked with her. He'd enjoyed a healthy sex life with Anju, had had many sexual encounters since she'd died, but with Dodi, the act seemed deeper, more mysterious, intense. The physical release wasn't the end goal. She wasn't a way to blow off steam. With Dodi, it was the journey, not the destination that was important.

And that was very, very new.

He couldn't help but compare her to Anju—his wife was the only long-term partner he'd had and, as such, his only reference.

He'd enjoyed Anju's astounding intellect and their

highbrow conversations about politics, neuroscience, chemistry and astronomy. But they'd never laughed or joked around, discussed the mundane and the ridiculous, the normal and the nonsensical. There was a good chance that he and Dodi would never talk about the latest brain-imaging techniques or scientific discoveries, but they could discuss books and music and movies, politics and religion.

She'd make him laugh, and curse, and she would challenge him to feel more, be more, *engage* more.

And that wasn't a bad thing.

He'd thought he'd been so clever, constructing his life and his marriage to be safe, to be stable. In trying to avoid drama, he'd created a life that was, in all honesty, stiflingly boring. It was hard to admit that he'd been living on the edge of life, scared to swim to the centre. In the middle of the pool of life were the currents, the whirlpools and rapids, where things got interesting. It was safe at the edges, but it was also deeply uninteresting, and mind-numbingly predictable.

The centre held energy, it demanded you engage, be present. Dodi was turning out to be his centre, his favourite whirlpool, the current taking him on a new journey.

Her dropping into his life, with her vibrant looks and personality, had flipped his world upside down and yeah, she was everything he needed. Up until now, he hadn't *lived* life, he'd operated to the side of it, scared to wade out of the shallows.

Sure, his childhood had been tough. He hated the

way his father had acted, and the way he had raised them…

But he wasn't his dad, didn't have to make the same choices his father had and wasn't obliged to *be* his father. His childhood was over, and he couldn't keep living in the past or letting his father and his actions affect what he did today, how he lived his life.

And, since he was going to be a father, he needed to teach his kid to be brave, to live authentically, to take chances, to engage with the world. If he kept himself separate, remained on the sidelines of life, then that was what his child would do too…

No, he wanted his child to grab life by the horns and go on a wild ride, skidding in at the end on a whoop and a grin, yelling that he'd had a hell of a ride.

Actually, that was how he wanted to be. He'd wasted so much time looking for trouble, trying to keep himself safe…and he was done. He wanted to live, dammit. Feel. Be present. If he was going to have another relationship, create a family, then he had to do it properly, go all in and skip the emotional guardrails and airbags. If he wanted to live the rest of his life with Dodi, with his kid, creating a life and a family with her, he needed to be brave, open, fully present, and God…emotionally available.

The thought made his hands tremble.

If he wanted the happy-ever-after with Dodi, he first had to get her to trust him. But she was as emotionally wary, as scarred as he was. Could they build something new, start afresh, or was he tilting at windmills, setting himself up for a sky-high fall?

He didn't know, couldn't predict the outcome. But

when faced with the alternative—living a half-life, with Dodi on the periphery of it—he knew that he had to take this huge, crazy, scary leap.

And hope like hell that Dodi would catch him.

'I do want to be part of the process. Don't doubt that, sweetheart. I'm not going anywhere.'

Dodi stood in her shower stall, her hands flat against the wall, her lips pursed, deep in thought as she remembered Jago's words from their intense conversation two weeks ago. Did she believe him? Would he stick around?

She trusted Jago, as much as she trusted anyone, and she knew he was a straight-shooting guy, someone who didn't mince words and who did what he said...

He was also considerate and thoughtful, and since telling him she was pregnant he'd shown her that he cared for her. He'd looked her car over, decided it needed new tyres, and loaned her another car while her tyres were being changed. While her car was in the workshop, he'd also arranged for it to have a top-to-bottom service. Frankly, she was surprised he hadn't replaced the thing!

Jabu, his butler, was now a frequent visitor to her house, always accompanied by a Hadleigh housemaid. She hadn't cleaned her house or done her laundry in over a month. Her freezer was stocked with nutritional meals, easy-to-heat food full of all the nutrients she and the baby needed.

Jago was taking care of her and, God help her, she liked it! She shouldn't, but she did. But she still harboured a deep-seated fear of being abandoned and couldn't shake the voice of doom that kept insisting that this couldn't last, that Jago would hurt and disappoint her. It was, after all, the pattern of her life.

She wasn't being fair to him. He hadn't done anything to deserve her mistrust and she wanted to enjoy their growing closeness, the intimacy that had sprung up between them. But something kept holding her back…

Her heart and her head were at war, that much was clear. Her heart was head-over-heels in love with the man, while her brain was asking if she was off her rocker. Her heart wanted to tell him how she felt about him, and her brain wanted to slap a gag over her mouth.

Her heart insisted she could trust him. Her brain was deeply concerned that she was losing her capacity for rational thought. She felt as if she was playing host to two squabbling teenagers, both determined to be in control, to have the upper hand.

She did love Jago but she also wanted to stay safe. She wanted him in her life, to share her life—for her to share his—but she didn't want to open herself up to being disappointed, to be let down by him. She wanted his beautiful body, to feel his touch every day and in every way, but she needed to keep her heart encased in Teflon. She wanted everything to change but she also wanted things to stay the same.

But she wasn't the only one with skin in the game, so what did Jago want? Did she even have the first clue? Dodi snapped her thumbnail against her front tooth, deep in thought.

He wasn't interested in love. He'd said as much.

He didn't want the messiness and the drama of being in a relationship. He'd married Anju to have a drama-free, cleverly constructed life with someone whose company he enjoyed, whose body he loved. They'd entered into a well-thought-out arrangement, and it seemed to have worked.

Why couldn't she and Jago have something similar?

She wasn't talking about marriage—that was too complicated—but maybe they could live together, sleep together, raise their child together. They could sleep in the same bed, have hot sex, which they both enjoyed.

And, if they felt like it, they could talk about their lives, thoughts, and feelings.

Could it work? Was she brave enough to suggest such a thing?

A hard rap on the bathroom door made her jump. She spun around as Jago opened the bathroom door and stepped inside, dressed in dark suit trousers that hugged his muscular thighs and a white button-down shirt that skated across his broad chest. A mint-green tie, still to be knotted, hung down his chest. He'd shaved and his hair was carefully tousled. Lord, he was hot.

Jago flashed her a smile. 'No, I'm not getting into the shower with you, temptress. I've got to get moving.'

His ability to read her mind still disconcerted her. Jago waited for her to turn off the water and then opened the shower door and handed her a towel. 'I'm running late but I need to talk to you before I go.'

She caught the worry in his eyes and frowned as

she wrapped the towel around her torso. She was about to ask him what was wrong, but he walked back into her bedroom. Concerned, Dodi quickly dried off, ran a comb through her hair and pulled on her dressing gown. In her bedroom, Jago stood by her window, frowning as he gulped from his steaming coffee cup. 'I made you some ginger tea.'

'Thank you,' she said, sitting down on the edge of the bed before picking up her cup. 'What's up? You're looking quite grim.'

'Have you seen the weather report this morning?'

He knew she hadn't. They'd woken up, rolled towards each other and made love. Then she'd dozed as he showered and changed. Then she'd showered…

Besides, she wasn't someone who routinely checked the weather. It was summer in Africa and that meant heat and the occasional thunderstorm. What was the point of routinely checking something she couldn't control?

'They are predicting a torrential downpour this afternoon, with the possibility of huge hail.' Right, Jago did check weather reports. That made sense, as he had a habit of scanning his world for potential disruptions and changes.

'It's going to cause havoc on the roads. I don't want you driving in it.'

She'd navigated the crazy roads of this city for a long time and she wasn't worried.

'Can you leave work early today?' Jago demanded, and Dodi bristled at the command she heard in his voice. 'They are expecting the worst of it to hit around six, but I'd prefer it if you were off the roads way before then.'

Dodi pushed her hand through her wet hair. 'I'll be fine, Jago. They always exaggerate!'

She could see the irritation in his eyes, the tension in his jaw. 'I don't want you driving in torrential rain,' he stated through gritted teeth. 'Close your business early and get home. Please.'

The *please* he uttered didn't detract from the force of his order. How she hated being told what to do, being made to do something she didn't want to do!

Deciding to play him at his own game, she tipped her head to the side and narrowed her eyes. 'Okay, then you get home before the storm strikes too. I don't want you driving in torrential rain either. Blow off your appointments and get home early.'

'I have a board meeting at five that's going to take about five or six hours—'

'Five or six hours? What are you discussing, how to rule the world?' she asked, trying to lighten the mood.

He didn't smile. 'Micah and I are presenting some new projects to the board, some of which will take the company in a whole new direction. It's a meeting that will have massive consequences for the company and will present some significant risks. It's probably the most important board meeting since my father died. But I wish we could delay it.'

'Why don't you?' Dodi asked.

'It's difficult to find a date that suits all the board members, and some of the projects are time-sensitive. If we don't get their approval tonight, we'll miss our window of opportunity,' he explained. 'I have to be there. It's vitally important.'

And her business was vitally important to her. 'I have brides coming in at four. I can't leave L&E either.'

Jago slammed his coffee cup down and rubbed his hands over his face. 'I just want you to be safe, dammit.'

'I'm a grown woman, Jago—I can make my own decisions about my business, my safety and my actions.'

'You're pregnant!' he yelled.

She was, but so what? 'I didn't lose my ability to act independently, or to think, when you impregnated me, Jago.'

He released a low growl and stomped over to the walk-in wardrobe, where he'd hung his suit jacket. He returned, pulling it on with jerky movements. 'I'm just trying to look after you, Elodie Kate! I'm concerned, that's all.'

She was pretty sure he was, but it felt as if he was trying to bend her to his will. Maybe she was overreacting, maybe not, but she couldn't allow him to bark orders at her and expect her to obey. She was perfectly capable of looking after herself, and she didn't need a big, bossy billionaire telling her what to do and how to do it! Jago stopped in front of her and glared down at her.

'Will you, at the very least, let me know your plans? I need to know when you leave and that you are safely home. I'll be in the board meeting, so I won't be able to respond, but I'll see your message.'

He still looked frustrated, but his suggestion was reasonable, so she nodded. 'Okay.'

Jago bent down and dropped a hard kiss on her mouth. 'It would be so much easier if you just did as I asked, Elodie Kate.'

'I'd bore you within a week if I did that,' Dodi informed him. *And I'd lose all respect for myself.* 'You should go, Jago—you said you're already late.'

Jago nodded and walked to the door. He placed his hand on the doorframe and looked back at her, his expression hesitant. 'I'll probably only make it home by midnight tonight, if I'm lucky. I'll see you later, okay?'

He thought of her home as his and she thought of his as hers. Was he, maybe, feeling something more for her? Could he, possibly, be having feelings for her? The thoughts made her stomach fizz, her brain a little fuzzy from happiness. She knew hope was dangerous, that she was setting herself up for disappointment, but Jago was a deliberate guy who was careful not to raise expectations. What he said, he meant…

'Do not drive in that storm!' he told her again, the command in his voice unmistakable, and her excitement fizzled and died. She heard the sound of his size thirteens running down her steps, the slam of her front door. Dodi shook her head, bewildered by their argument, the confusion it raised, and the highs and the lows of their interactions. Ten minutes ago, she'd been considering a life with this man, living together, trying to build something. She'd thought that he might be feeling the same, just a little. But then his commands and demands, his banked frustration at not getting his way, made her wonder if she could be with him, whether they had a future together.

It made her question whether he'd ever consider her an equal partner and not someone under his protection, someone whose life he wanted to manipulate and direct, someone who'd manoeuvre her into situations she didn't want or choose. And if she didn't do as he wanted, if she baulked too often, would he decide that she wasn't worth his effort and time? Would he think that his life was better off without her in it? Would he abandon her, leaving her holding her shattered heart?

Maybe it was better not to take that chance, maybe it was better to keep her emotional distance, to erect her emotional guardrails again.

Dodi flopped back on her bed and turned her head to look out of her window. She scowled at the blue sky. There was a storm on the way, and not just in the meteorological sense.

CHAPTER ELEVEN

DODI, HER HEART in her mouth, hands wet with perspiration, peered through the driving rain, and crawled down Jago's street, looking for the gates to Hadleigh House. It was shortly after six and yes, the storm had rolled in, more vicious than she'd expected. Jago had called it and she wished she'd left work early because the visibility was dreadful, the roads were river-like and there was still, so she'd been told, an excellent chance of hail.

Dodi heard the sharp crack of lightning, felt the fizz of electricity and jumped at the boom of thunder. She needed to get off the road as soon as possible… where the hell was Hadleigh House?

She'd been annoyed earlier when a Le Roux intern dropped off an envelope from Jago containing the remote control to an electric gate and a set of keys.

His terse note was not a heartfelt love letter.

If you're going to be stubborn and stay at work, at least drive to Hadleigh House instead of trying to make your way across town to your place. It's closer. Let me know when you leave and when you arrive. Also, Jabu is on holiday, so the house is empty. Alarm code below.

She'd been leaving work when the heavens opened and she quickly decided that driving to Jago's house was the sensible option. She was stubborn but not, she hoped, stupid.

Dodi gripped her steering wheel tighter and narrowed her eyes, trying to get her bearings. Forty-eight, fifty…she was getting close. Her windscreen wipers were operating at full speed and her windshield was steaming up, and she lifted her hand to clear a small circle in front of her. As she caught sight of the gates to Jago's house, she heard the sharp ping of something hard hitting her roof and she cursed. Hail! Dammit!

She swung into Jago's driveway and fumbled for the remote control to open the gates, cursing the pebble-sized hailstones bouncing off the bonnet. Her car was going to look like a golf ball after this.

The gates opened and Dodi crawled up the drive. She usually parked to the side of the house but tonight she was going to get as close as she could to the entrance, and when the hailstones stopped she'd run up the stone stairs and into Jago's house.

Dodi waited for five minutes before the worst of the hail stopped. The rain was still bucketing down, and lightning and thunder still chased each other around the sky. She'd get wet—why wasn't she one of those organised people who kept an umbrella in her car?—but that was okay. It was just water. She'd survive. Deciding to leave her bag in her car, Dodi wrapped her phone into the hem of her shirt to protect it from getting soaked, grabbed Jago's bunch of keys and pushed open her car door, fighting the wind wanting to slam it closed.

Bending her head, she ran through the hard rain, wincing as the needle-hard droplets slammed into her face and plastered her hair and clothes to her body. By the time she reached the stone steps, she was soaked through. She slowed down as she hurried up the steps, wiping her eyes and pushing back her wet hair. The huge front door was just there, and, behind it, warmth and safety. She'd send a message to Jago telling him she was safe and then she'd dry off, make herself some tea. And when the storm died down she'd take a long, hot shower. Bliss…she couldn't wait.

Dodi stepped onto the slate floor of the portico, took two steps, maybe three, and then her feet slid out from under her and her butt slammed down, bouncing off the tiles. Her back hit the floor and then her head. Burning pain ratcheted up her spine and she released a high-pitched scream, which was immediately sucked into the storm.

Her last thoughts as she passed out were a quick prayer that her baby was okay. She needed Jago…and she needed him *now.*

Jago opened the door to Dodi's private hospital room and leaned his shoulder on the doorframe, happy to watch her sleep. The past twelve hours had been some of the worst of his life and he'd felt as though his heart had started and restarted a hundred times.

He never, ever wanted to relive last night. And he'd

do everything in his power to make sure that Dodi would always be safe and protected, dammit.

He could've lost her last night and the thought made his heart drop like a stone to his shoes and his throat close. It was time they stopped mucking around and she moved in with him, where he could look after her and love her.

Because love her he did. More than he'd ever believed possible. He'd been fighting his feelings, ignoring the sensations he didn't recognise—and therefore weren't, in his rational mind, valid—determined to keep things between them under control.

Her falling, cracking her head—the possibility of losing her—was a wake-up-and-face-the-music call. For the first time in his life, he felt as if his life was incomplete, that up until now he'd been unaware of the Dodi-sized hole in his life. He needed her: she made him a better man. A life without her in it was a wasteland, grey, wet and utterly miserable. She was light, colour, fun, laughter…love.

She was his everything. Dodi sighed, her eyes opened and she turned her head to the door, a soft smile on her face. 'Hi,' she murmured.

Jago walked over to the bed, sat down next to her and stroked his thumb over her still pale cheek. 'Hi back. How are you feeling?'

'A bit of a headache…' Dodi's eyes widened, and she shot up, panic on her face. 'The baby…is our baby okay?'

He gripped her shoulders, gently squeezed and bent his head so that he could look directly into her eyes. 'The baby is fine, Dodi. Relax.'

It took her a few deep breaths for his news to make sense. 'Are you sure?' she demanded, her voice shrill.

'Very. They did an ultrasound, and all is well.'

The panic in her eyes receded and was quickly replaced by tears. Of gratitude, he presumed. She flopped back on the pillow and closed her eyes. 'Thank God, thank God.'

He wholeheartedly agreed. Thank God. Jago found the remote control and lifted the bed so that Dodi sat upright. He resumed his place next to her and placed his hand on her thigh. 'Don't you remember having the ultrasound?'

The doctor said that some of her memories might be fuzzy as she'd cracked her head quite hard. She hadn't needed stitches but she did have a large goose egg on the back of her head.

Dodi shrugged. 'I remember bits and pieces of last night, not much. I remember running up the steps, slipping, my butt hitting the floor and how sore it was.'

'You bruised your coccyx and smacked the back of your head,' Jago told her. 'You have a minor concussion.'

'That explains the headache,' Dodi commented. 'Who found me?'

'I did. You didn't let me know that you were home and I felt uneasy.' Jago brushed her hair off her forehead and tucked it behind her ear. 'I couldn't concentrate, at all, so I excused myself from the board meeting and left the room.'

Dodi winced. 'Were they mad?'

He shrugged. 'It was at a crucial point in the presentation, so they weren't impressed, but I couldn't continue, I couldn't focus on anything but my rising dread. I tried to call you but your phone just rang and rang.'

'I'm sorry, I didn't mean to scare you.'

'You took ten years off my life,' Jago ruefully told her. 'I used an app to find your phone, saw that you were at my house, but you weren't inside because the alarm was still on. I checked the camera feeds and saw you lying outside the front door. My heart stopped.'

She winced and gestured for him to continue. 'I called for an ambulance, told Micah I was leaving and raced home.'

Despite the torrential rain, he'd made the trip home in ten minutes instead of his usual fifteen. It had been a hair-raising trip, not knowing how seriously she was injured.

'You left your important board meeting for me?' Dodi asked, linking her fingers in his.

He'd move mountains for her if he could.

'I thought it crucially important that you were there.'

Not as important as her. He shrugged. 'Micah handled it.'

'And did they vote for your changes?' Dodi asked, tipping her head to the side.

He didn't know and didn't much care. Not at this moment, anyway. She was all that was important, his entire focus. 'I have no idea.'

Dodi sighed, sat up and draped her arms around his neck, snuggling in. 'I remember you looking over me last night, your hand stroking my hair back. I was so very glad to see you, to have you there.'

His hand drifted up and down her slim back. 'I'll always be there, Elodie Kate. And last night made me realise that it was ridiculous for us to live apart. I can't do that any more—I need to have you close by, need to be able to protect you.' He shuddered. 'I can't go through that again.'

She rubbed her hand over his back. 'It was an accident, Jago and I'm fine. The baby is fine.'

This time. He couldn't lose her, wouldn't take that risk. 'The doctor said that you can be discharged but he wants you taking it easy for the rest of the week.'

She nodded, wincing. 'I can do that.'

Progress, Jago thought on a smile. 'Then let's get you dressed, and I'll take you home.'

Dodi nodded and pushed back the bedcovers, trying to hide her wince. 'I can't wait to be in my bed, sleeping on my pillow.'

He shook his head. 'You're not going home. You're coming back to my place. Jabu and one of the maids are packing up your clothes and toiletries as we speak, and when you are up to it you can tell me what furniture you want to be moved to Hadleigh House. I know it's Lily's house and you might not want to sell it but maybe you can rent it out, partially furnished. Or we can store the stuff you don't want to get rid of.'

She stared at him, a frown pulling her eyebrows together. 'I'm sorry, I don't understand.'

Jago dumped the small overnight bag he'd brought with him, containing a change of her clothes. He pulled out a pair of loose summer trousers, a comfortable T-shirt, clean underwear. 'What's to understand? You're moving into my place, with me.'

Her fists bunched and the colour drained from her face. Her eyes turned a deep, hard blue and it was at that moment that Jago realised that in his haste to have her with him, to look after her and to love her, he'd badly miscalculated. He'd made a major decision without her input....

He rubbed his jaw, his mind going at a mile a minute, trying to work out how he could extract himself from the quicksand he'd blindly walked into.

'Please, please tell me that you didn't just say what I thought you did. You couldn't possibly have done all that without consulting me,' Dodi said, her voice ultra-polite. 'I told you how I feel about being pushed into situations not of my choosing, how I hate being manoeuvred, so you couldn't have done something so idiotic.'

He had. Jesus. Why hadn't he remembered that?

Because all he wanted this morning—after a night of sitting by her bedside staring at her, imagining a life without her in it—was to bind her to him, to hold her and keep her and protect her. She'd scared him senseless, and he'd just wanted her with him.

He hadn't thought further than meeting that objective. Stupid. So stupid.

Dodi bit down on her bottom lip and stared at her tightly linked hands. 'For a minute there, I was so happy, despite feeling like I've been run over by a truck. Our baby is fine and you prioritised me over your very important board meeting. You came to find me, and you were there for me. I felt at peace, knowing and trusting that you would be there for me, that you'd never let me down.'

But...because, hell, there was a great big but to follow.

Dodi rubbed her hands over her face and when she dropped them she looked stricken. 'But despite that, you still don't *get* it, you don't *get* me. I promised myself I'd never allow myself to be pushed around again, would never permit someone to force me in a direction I didn't want to go.'

God, he was a moron. Why hadn't he considered that? What the hell was wrong with him?

Dodi met his eyes, and hers were filled with pain. And not because she was physically hurting. 'Give me a reason why you'd do this, Jago. Please.'

Jago cursed the fact that he had no defence, that he could find no words to make it right. He wanted to tell her that he loved her, that he'd acted out of panic and passion, that he couldn't imagine not having her in his life so he'd taken steps to get her there. But the words stuck on his tongue, and he was unable to push them past his teeth. He'd never told a woman that he loved her, didn't know how. He could negotiate multi-billion deals, had, reputedly, balls of steel, but not when it came to love.

He didn't know how to explain, what to say. What words to use. How to *do* this.

Dodi shook her head, closed her eyes. 'This isn't going to work, Jago, it can't work. We've been kidding ourselves, confused by the attraction between us. You need to have control, and to plan and protect and I can't or won't be controlled, shoved into situations you think are best for me.' Dodi's voice was soft but strong and very, very resolute. She slid out of bed, gathered her clothes and nodded to the small bathroom. 'I'm going to change and you're going to leave.'

He opened his mouth to tell her that she didn't have a ride home, but she held up her hand and shook her head. 'I'm going to call Thadie, ask her to come and get me. And no, I won't badmouth you to your sister. But you'd better call Jabu and tell him to replace my stuff, and inform him, and anyone else you told, that I will *not* be moving in with you. Not today, tomorrow or any time in the future.'

Well, that sounded bloody final. Jago rubbed the area above his heart and watched her walk into the bathroom and close the door behind her. When he heard the lock engage, he knew that it was over and that he'd lost the only woman he'd ever loved.

And he'd done it within two months. He knew how to work fast, but that had to be a record…

Dodi walked into her busy salon and handed the sample dress to a consultant, watching the bride's eyes light up when she presented the frothy princess-style ballgown. She danced on the spot and her smile was as big as the sun.

She ran a reverent hand over the puffy tulle, her expression wondrous. 'I've been dreaming of this moment since I was eight. Trying on a dress, looking like a fairy-tale bride.'

God, another one who was so caught up in the nuptials and wasn't looking beyond the big day. Dodi handed her a tight smile and did an internal eye roll. 'I think it will look wonderful on you.'

She watched the bride walk towards the dressing

room and rubbed the region above her heart. Since leaving Jago's house nearly a week ago, her heart felt heavy and full. She had acid in her stomach, and tears gathered in her throat. She missed him, so much. She felt like she was walking around with a red-hot heart, one that was, at all times, one bump away from disintegrating.

'She might be young but she's not rushing into this with her eyes closed.'

Dodi turned to look at the bride's mother, sitting on the two-seater sofa next to where she was standing. She hadn't even noticed the well-dressed woman sitting there, hair and make-up perfect. What else hadn't she noticed while she was wallowing around in her Jago-induced funk?

Dodi pulled up a polite smile. 'I'm sorry, I don't know what you mean.'

The older woman cocked her head to the side. 'Now, that's not true. You think she's only thinking of the wedding, hasn't paid any attention to being married, to being in a committed relationship for the rest of her life…'

Dodi rubbed her fingers across her forehead and gestured to the seat next to her. 'Do you mind?'

'Not at all. I'm Dee.'

'My name is Dodi. I own this salon.'

Dee peered at her. 'Are you Lily's granddaughter? You look like her!'

Dodi smiled. 'I am. I inherited the store when she died.'

Dee scrunched up her nose. 'I'm so sorry to hear that. Lily fitted me with my wedding dress and she's the reason why I'm celebrating my thirtieth wedding anniversary this year.'

Dodi turned to face her, her attention snagged. She loved hearing stories about her grandmother. 'Really? What did she do?'

'She talked me out of my grand five-hundred-person wedding,' Dee said, her eyes alight with amusement.

Dodi's mouth fell open. 'What?'

'Mmm. I was one of those brides, so caught up with the wedding and the pomp and ceremony, that I didn't think of anything else. Your grandmother sat me down, asked me about my fiancé, what he did, what he liked, his hobbies and his politics. I couldn't answer any of her probing questions about him and it irritated me.

'Then one day my then fiancé's brother gave me a lift to this salon and walked in with me. Your gran asked about him and I could tell her his favourite colour, that he hates olives, that he's allergic to bees and that Faulkner is his favourite author. She let me rattle on about Grant and, without her saying a word, I realised I was marrying the wrong brother.' She winced. 'It took about three years before the family forgave me for ditching one brother for the other. Four years later I returned here to buy dress number two.'

'That's such a lovely story,' Dodi said, conscious of how much she missed Lily. What she wouldn't do right now for one of her hugs.

Dee crossed her legs. 'I spent quite a bit of time here, back in the day. I used to make excuses to come here, to be around Lily. I felt a real connection to her, and I loved listening to her stories, hearing about her life.'

Dodi felt tears gathering in her throat. 'What sort of things did she tell you?' she asked.

'Ah, she'd tell me about her childhood, her friends and how much she loved the store. But the stories I loved best were about Tim, her husband.'

The grandfather she had never met. 'They had a fairy-tale romance. I've seen pictures of him, and he was good-looking, as well. I've always imagined him to be the perfect groom, an absolute Prince Charming,' Dodi said.

Dee widened her eyes. 'Are we talking about the same guy? Because that wasn't how your grandmother saw him.'

Dodi frowned, puzzled. 'Lily adored Tim, she told me that often. They were deeply in love.' She couldn't bear it if the *one* love affair she believed in wasn't true. She wouldn't be able to cope with knowing that!

'Oh, I agree with that, they were in love. But your grandfather wasn't anything like Prince Charming,' Dee explained.

'Really?'

'He was, as Lily often said, the strong but silent type. He found it very difficult to express his emotions and she said that he wasn't good at verbalising his feelings. Tim didn't drop *I love yous*, but Lily had no doubt she was loved, deeply and completely.'

Dodi was fascinated by this insight into her grandmother's life. 'Did she tell you how she knew he loved her?'

Dee smiled. 'I asked her the same question and I'll

never forget her answer…she told me that love sometimes speaks in different languages. Someone might not say "I love you" but they might check whether you've eaten, or whether you had a good sleep, offer to help when they see you are struggling. She said that some people's love was spoken through actions, not words.'

Dodi stared at her, a bankload of pennies dropping into her brain. Jago didn't speak of love, had never suggested or hinted that he was in love with her, but his actions spoke a million words. He often checked in to see how she was feeling, allowed her to sleep when she was tired, brought her ginger tea when she was feeling nauseous. He sent his staff to clean her house and do her laundry, trying to lighten her load. He made sure her car was in peak condition, that her tyres were new and that everything was reliable and safe. He'd been insanely worried about her driving in that horrible storm, and he'd rushed out of a crucial, company-defining board meeting to check on her.

His actions spoke of his love…

But he'd tried to rearrange her life and wanted to shove her into a situation without consulting her. She'd been incredibly angry because she'd *told* him she loathed being placed in situations not of her choosing, where she had no control. He'd forged ahead anyway…

But maybe, just maybe, Jago had been terrified by the events of the previous night and he'd been scared, of losing her, losing what they had. It was in his nature to scan his world for things to go wrong and he'd seen the possible consequences of the storm and he'd asked her to take precautions. She'd ignored him, and when his fears came true he reacted by trying to control the situation, by gathering her closer, fuelled by his need to protect her…

Because he'd been petrified of losing her.

Could that be true? Or was she conning herself, desperate to find an excuse to be with him again?

Dee cleared her throat. 'One more thing, Dodi. My daughter isn't a silly bride—'

Dodi winced, excruciatingly embarrassed. 'God, I'm so sorry—'

Dee placed her hand on hers and squeezed. 'I'm not trying to make you feel bad, I just want to explain why your assumption was so very wrong. Courtney has been with Drake for eight years and he stood by and supported her while she underwent a mastectomy and a year of chemotherapy. He made her laugh and held her while she cried. He made her feel beautiful when her hair fell out, before she had reconstructive surgery. And Courts, well, she came face to face with her mortality and she wants to grab life by its neck and live it. But she wants to do it with Drake.'

Dodi felt tears burn her eyes and placed her hand on her chest, as if to stop her heart from climbing out through her ribs. Okay, maybe she did judge her brides far too quickly. And, obviously, erroneously. 'I'm so sorry. I shouldn't have rushed to judgement.'

Dee's smile was soft and full of sweetness. 'Your grandmother loved weddings, but she didn't wear rose-coloured glasses. She knew who would make it and who wouldn't…what it took to be happy,' Dee told her, giving her hand a quick squeeze. 'She was a wise woman, your Lily.'

Dodi nodded, smiled and stood up. 'Thank you for sharing your memories of her with me. It means a lot. And I do hope you visit again, with or without your lovely daughter.'

Her eyes burning, Dodi walked away from Dee, blinking furiously. She turned down the passageway, marked Staff Only, and leaned back against the wall, able to see her busy shop, her consultants, and her excited brides.

Did she hate the shop and her job because she didn't believe in love or was it because she *did* believe in love and she hated the fact that it never stuck around for her? Was she jealous of her brides' happiness and security? Did she actually, somewhere deep down, want to be married, be part of a couple, be wrapped up in another person, in every way possible?

Would she want to be married to Jago?

Hell yes. A thousand times.

So maybe it was time to stop fudging, to tell herself the truth without embellishments, without trying to protect herself. She loved Jago, with every atom of her being, every cell, every breath she took. And she did trust him because he'd shown her, time and time again, that he was there for her, that she was a priority.

She finally understood his love language…

More than anything, she wanted their lives, hearts, bodies and feelings to be tangled up in each other. She wanted to be in love, a bride excited to get married, to be part of a couple, to start a life with someone she adored.

One of her consultants hurried past her and Dodi

reached out to stop her. She braked, turned and smiled. 'How can I help, Dodi?'

'There's a bride in changing room number three by the name of Courtney. Her mum's name is Dee.'

Her assistant nodded. 'Dark hair, huge smile?'

Dodi nodded. 'Yeah. She's trying on a Pablo dress, but I don't think she can afford it. She'll probably settle for a cheaper dress in the same style. Sell her Pablo's sample dress, at cost.'

She saw her assistance's confusion, understandable because they never sold the sample dresses, as the brides needed to use them to make their initial choices. She'd just spent a little under forty thousand with Pablo. He could send her another dress in the same style.

Her assistant nodded. 'You're the boss.'

Yes, she was. And this was her business, one that helped make a bride feel beautiful, contributed to a magical start to what was supposed to be a magical life. Oh, it wouldn't be, not every day, but one started as one meant to go on. She wasn't ever going to sell or dispense of Lily's business, so maybe it was time to change her attitude towards it and try to love it instead.

And if she was going to fix her relationship with Love & Enchantment, then she was also going to fix her relationship with Jago. Or, at the very least, she was going to try.

CHAPTER TWELVE

A FEW DAYS LATER, Jago stepped onto the entertainment area at Hadleigh House and saw his twin sitting on the edge of the pool, his feet in the water. They'd returned from a ten-kilometre run a half-hour ago and, like him, Micah had showered and changed into a pair of shorts and a T-shirt.

'Want a beer?' Jago asked.

'Sure.'

Jago took two bottles out of the fridge and walked over to where Micah sat, dropping down to sit next to him, feet in the water. He handed over his beer, placed his bottle on the paving next to him and leaned back on his hands. Night had fallen and he could hear the sound of the cicadas and the frogs. It was a stunning night and he wished he were spending it with Dodi and not his twin. He liked Micah but…

'Thank you for running the board meeting the other night and convincing the board to go along with our plans. That was all you, and I am grateful.' Micah had done a hell of a job and the future direction of Le Roux International, cleaner and greener, was all down to his brother.

Micah tapped the neck of his beer bottle against Jago's. 'I'm not just a pretty face,' he quipped.

He most certainly was not.

'I know you have a lot going on, but have you found a venue yet for Thadie's wedding?' Jago asked, rolling his tense shoulders.

It was still light enough for him to see Micah's wince. 'No. Maybe.'

Jago lifted his eyebrows at Micah's non-answer. His brother was normally more decisive. 'What does that mean?'

'It means that Ella, the event planner I'm working with, might have a lead on a property that could be very suitable, but it isn't currently being used as a wedding venue,' Micah told him.

Jago had a million questions and started to ask the first one that came to mind when Micah held up his hand. 'Not in the mood for the third degree, Jay. You'll know, as soon as I do, as soon as Thadie does, whether it's an option or not.'

His brother looked shattered, Jago realised. Almost as tired as he did. 'Everything okay?'

Micah shrugged and Jago knew, without his saying anything, that things weren't okay, but Micah wasn't ready to talk. Not yet.

But he was. He felt like a volcano ready to erupt and he needed to talk to someone. No, he needed to talk to his brother, his twin, the person who knew him best. But Micah beat him to the punch. 'Can you believe that by this time next year you're going to be a dad?'

He couldn't. But he could. Both at the same time. He took a long sip of his beer, trying to get his erratic pulse under control. 'I can't wrap my head around it, to be honest.'

'You've always said that you didn't want kids, so are you okay with it?'

Very okay. 'I am. Dodi made me realise that I'm not Theo, that I don't have to be the father he was.'

Micah nodded. 'Just do the exact opposite to what he did, and you'll be awesome.'

That was the plan. Jago felt Micah's eyes on his face, could almost hear the wheels turning in his brain. He braced himself for his next question. 'I haven't seen Dodi around lately. Everything okay between you two?'

'No.'

Micah grimaced. 'What happened?'

Jago released a long sigh. 'I messed up. The morning after the storm, I arranged, without talking to her, for her to move in here, with me.'

Micah scratched his chin. 'Sorry, but I'm not seeing the problem here.'

'What you don't know is that Dodi has a deep-seated, understandable hatred of having her life arranged without her input. She was furious that I didn't consult her before sending Jabu over to pack up her stuff. She told me that it would never work between us and basically, dumped me.'

Micah's eyebrows shot up. 'Really?'

No, he was making things up as he went along… 'Yeah, *really*.'

Micah held up a placating hand. 'So your controlling behaviour finally came back to bite you?' he asked, amusement coating his words.

'I'm not controlling…' Jago's words trailed off and he dropped his head. 'Of course I am, but I don't do it to be a jerk. I just wanted what I thought was best for her. I'm crazy in love with her and I genuinely believe that living here, with me, would be the best thing for her and the baby.'

'Did you tell her that?'

'No.'

'So what did you say to her?' Micah asked.

Jago looked away. 'Nothing. I couldn't find the words. I just let her walk away.'

Micah released a low, pained groan and buried his head in his hands. 'Jago, seriously? What is wrong with you?'

'I tried to do the right thing with the best intentions, but it backfired. Maybe it's the wrong time, she's the wrong person. Maybe I'm just really, really bad at this.'

'I only agree with your last statement,' Micah informed him.

Jago shrugged. 'The more it means, the harder it is to say. Dad was a master of words, but he treated people terribly, especially those he was supposed to love. I never wanted to be like him, so I hold my words in, and it's become a habit.'

'What do you want to do, Jago? What do *you* want from *her*?'

Time to get real, he thought. Jago lifted his beer bottle and took a long sip. 'I want the emotional connection, to be able to love her, for her to be my wife in every way, good, bad and ugly. I want to spend my life talking to her, loving her, protecting her and our child, and the other kids I want to have with her!'

His voice was climbing higher and higher, and by the end of his sentence he was practically shouting.

'Don't you think Dodi needs to hear this, not me?' Micah nudged him with his shoulder. 'Let me put it another way… She can't read your mind, Jago, and even I find it difficult to read your feelings and we rented a womb together! Trust me, she has no idea that you love her. And by not consulting her about moving in, it looks like you don't give a damn about her past and that her feelings aren't valid or important. You are such a useless communicator, twin,' Micah added.

He was. And by not being brave enough to tell her the truth, the whole truth, to be vulnerable, he'd not only hurt her but also disrespected her. And that was utterly unacceptable.

'I need to talk to her,' Jago told Micah, sounding a little stunned.

'I think that's a damn good idea,' Micah replied. Then he lifted his empty beer bottle. 'But before you rush off, can you get me another beer?'

Where are you right now?

Dodi, about to get in her car after dinner at Thadie's house, looked at the message from Jago. She'd been trying to find her courage to contact him for days but kept finding excuses not to. She was tired, she was busy, she wasn't ready.

But what she was, was a complete coward. She was

still terrified of love, still scared of making a mistake, of being hurt.

But he'd reached out first. Why?

Dodi's heart lurched when her phone rang and his number popped up on her screen. She'd just been thinking about him…okay, in fairness, she was never *not* thinking about him. Waving at Thadie through the window, she pulled away, her phone tucked between her ear and shoulder.

'Jago?'

'Don't give me a hard time, just tell me where you are,' Jago said. God, he sounded…luscious.

She could argue but she didn't have the energy. 'I'm leaving Thadie's. Why?'

'I was going to ask you if I could come over to your place, but, since you are down the road, it would be quicker if you came here.'

Her heart jumped at the thought. She missed him, wanted to see him, wanted to inhale his amazing scent, lose herself in his eyes and his arms. 'Um…why?'

Jago didn't answer straight away, and when he did his voice sounded rough. 'Because I need to talk to you, and I'd prefer to do it now rather than make a long drive across town to talk to you in forty-five minutes.'

Dodi approached the end of Thadie's drive and hesitated. Left to go home or right to go to Hadleigh House?

'Are you coming or not?' Jago asked, his tone gentle but utterly determined. 'If not, I'll see you at your place.'

Dodi frowned. 'It's that important?'

'Anything to do with you, or us, is important,' Jago

quietly told her. 'Please come, Elodie Kate. I can't do another week like this last one, another minute.'

It was the please that did it, the sadness she heard in his voice. 'Okay. I'll be there in a minute or two.'

She heard his relieved sigh. 'The code for the gate is the same. Come in via the side door and I'll be in my apartment waiting for you.'

'Okay.'

A couple of minutes later, Dodi parked her car in its usual spot under the willow tree and, leaving her bag and phone in the car, walked up to the side entrance and tested the handle to the door. It was unlocked, so she stepped into his house and immediately turned to walk up the old servants' passage. Could it only be ten weeks since she'd first walked up these stairs, her hand in his? So much had happened in those few short weeks: she'd fallen pregnant and fallen in love with Jago.

And, strangely, fallen back in…well, not love but like with her little store.

Since her chat with Dee, she'd stopped judging her brides and was actively trying to learn their stories. She was asking them about their lives and the men they were going to marry.

Oh, she still encountered the occasional shallow-as-a-puddle entitled bride-to-be, but most of her clients were normal women, excited, nervous, insecure. Some of them were downright petrified of the massive decision they were making. It was weird but their nervousness and insecurities made her feel calmer, better, more accepting of herself.

Everyone had their issues…they were all human with human fears. As was she.

Reaching the landing, Dodi wiped her sweaty hands on her white shorts and headed for his door. She lifted her hand to knock, but before her fist made contact the door swung open and Jago gripped her wrist and pulled her into the room.

She bumped up against his chest, releasing a tiny squeal of surprise, but before she could say anything he took her mouth in a dazzling, desperate, so-good-to-see-you kiss. Dodi melted against him, wound her arms around his neck and fell into his kiss, her tongue dancing with his.

His arms were where she needed, *wanted* them to be.

It was Jago who broke their kiss, who pulled back and rested his forehead against hers, breathing heavily.

Dodi lifted her hand to her mouth. 'What was that?' she asked, panting.

'That was my way of telling you I miss you, that the last week has been hell, that I can't last a day without having you in my arms.'

Dodi blinked and blinked again, not recognising the need in Jago's voice, the blatant emotion. 'You missed me?' she asked.

'Every minute, every day,' Jago assured her, holding both her hands in his. 'I've been comprehensively useless at work, grumpy as hell and haven't been able to concentrate on anything.'

Dodi tried to process his words as he led her to the sofa and gestured for her to sit. Right, it was obvious that he'd missed her but as what? Did he miss his lover, the sex? Or did he miss *her*? There was a massive gulf between the two.

Dodi perched on the edge of the leather seat and draped one leg over her trembling knee. She forced herself to look at him and ask the question that was burning on her lips. 'Are we talking about you missing the sex we shared, Jago?'

He frowned at her before scratching the underside of his chin. 'Of course I miss the sex. We are brilliant together.'

Dodi's heart sank and she stared down at the carpet, her eyes burning with tears. What an idiot. What had she expected him to say? That he missed her laugh, and smile, missed talking to her?

'That came out wrong,' Jago said on a heavy sigh. He sat on the seat next to her and shook his head. 'You know, I'm pretty good at words. I can hold conversations, generally get my point across without misunderstandings, but when it comes to you and feelings I'm useless. My words get jumbled and I either say something I don't mean or don't say anything at all…'

'Are we still talking about you missing sex?' Dodi asked, puzzled.

He sighed and shook his head. 'I'll get back to that in a minute, but first…' He shoved his hands into his hair, his eyes filled with emotion. 'I messed up at the hospital. I was tired, scared and emotional. I wanted you with me and I made that happen without taking your feelings or opinion into account. That was wrong of me, and I will never do that again.'

She wanted to believe him, she did. 'Never is a long time, Jago.'

'I promise, Elodie Kate. And I don't make promises easily and often.'

The knots around her heart started to loosen and she took in the first deep breaths for hours, days.

Jago rubbed his hands over his face before dropping them to dangle them between his knees, his face turned to look at her. 'As I was saying earlier about the sex…yes, I miss sleeping with you, but I miss waking up with you more. I miss hearing about your day and your crazy brides, seeing your smile and have been irrationally worried about whether you were eating enough, sleeping, taking your vitamins. I love the sex, Dodi, but I love you more.'

His words were sweet, a balm to her scoured soul. He'd mentioned her smile, was worried about her… wait!

What? Had she heard him correctly?

'Did you just tell me you love me?' Dodi demanded, her voice nearly drowned out by the roaring in her ears. She must've heard wrong. Jago didn't believe in love.

'Of course I love you,' he stated calmly. 'I think I have since the first moment I kissed you in your salon. Maybe even when I kissed you all those years ago.'

Right, she'd fallen down a rabbit hole. 'You don't believe in love, remember?' Dodi told him, scooting away from him and holding out her hands.

'I do when it comes to you.'

Dodi stood up and started to pace the area next to the sofa. She waved her hands in the air. 'I'm feeling a bit overwhelmed here, Jago!'

Jago leaned back into the sofa and placed his bare

ankle on his knee. 'Tough,' he gently said, smiling. 'And, at the risk of overwhelming you some more, I don't want a loveless, tidy union with you, I want a messy one.'

'A messy one?' And yes, she really should stop repeating his words.

'I want the fights and the hugs, the laughter and the disagreements. I want the drama love brings, the excitement you bring to my life. I most definitely do not want a quiet life. Not with you.'

'I… What…? You're not making any sense!' Dodi wailed.

'I am and that's what's scaring you,' Jago calmly told her. 'You're scared, just as I am, of being with me, of loving me, of being in a relationship that makes us feel like we're riding a roller coaster. You're scared of being hurt, of trusting another man, another person. Scared that I will disappoint you and hurt you.'

All true, every word.

'I won't, you know. Hurt you or disappear on you or disappoint you, not in any of the big ways. Oh, I'm going to mess up, of that I am sure, but I will always be in your corner, Elodie Kate. I will always be there, standing by your side, carrying you when you need me to, standing behind you if you don't. I'll be the rock you need.'

Dodi lifted her fist to her mouth, startled to find tears running down her cheeks. 'Don't… Jago, please.'

Jago stood up and walked towards her, his thumb brushing the tears off her cheek. 'Don't what? Love you? Too late for that. Stand behind you? I'm going to do that whether you marry me or not. Even if you can't love me, you're the mother of my child and I'll do anything and everything to give you what you need, including my friendship and protection.'

Dodi looked up at him, his lovely face blurry from her tears. She sniffed. 'You want to marry me?'

'More than anything in the world, sweetheart.'

'But *why*?'

'Because with you I feel like I'm Jago, not the corporate shark or Theo Le Roux's son or Micah's twin. I feel like me. You make me better, lighter, so damn happy.'

She bit down on her bottom lip. 'So, this has nothing to do with the baby?'

He shook his head. 'I'm excited, still a little scared about becoming a father, but right now I'm talking about you and me. And our feelings for each other.' He pulled a face. 'Though so far I've been rambling on, and you've mostly just repeated my words.'

Dodi winced. 'I have, haven't I?'

'Well, here are some words I wish you'd repeat… I love you too, Jago.'

Dodi tipped her head to the side, not fooled by his small smile, the cockiness on his face. His eyes reflected his worry that she didn't love him back. The muscle in his jaw told her how tense he was. He was uncertain, feeling vulnerable, scared of her answer. Seeing this big, bold, tough-as-leather man vulnerable brought home the reality of his words. He did love her, he did want to be with her. He would stand beside her, next to her, he wanted to do life with her.

All he needed was her trust and her assurance that she loved him too.

'I trust you, Jago.'

She saw hope jump into his eyes. 'You do?'

'I do. With my heart and my feelings, with my opinions and my life. Lily was my rock, the one person I trusted implicitly, no questions asked, with every fibre of my being. But I've realised that you show your love through actions. You've shown me that you love me, in so many different ways. I do trust you, Jago, just as I did her.' She saw his Adam's apple bob, saw the hint of moisture in his eyes and, feeling brave, and powerful, and oh-so-feminine, she placed a hand on his heart.

There were more words she needed to say. Good words, strong words. Important words. 'I love your body. I love making love with you. I'm already crazy about our child. But you, Jago, *you* make my heart sing. I look at you and I feel both excited and content, jittery and calm. And I feel love, so much of it. You own my heart, Jago, and I love you.'

Jago's big hand covered her cheek. 'Sweetheart... those words... I didn't think I needed them, and I didn't, not from anyone else but you.'

Dodi's bottom lip wobbled. 'Did you...did you mean it?'

Jago lifted his eyebrows. 'Mean what?' he asked, his eyes dancing with happiness and amusement.

'What you said about wanting to marry me?' Dodi asked in a small voice. Was she pushing too hard again? Asking for too much too quickly?

'Did you want me to mean it?' Jago asked her, his voice suddenly serious.

She looked up at him, doubts swirling. Then she realised that she couldn't keep hiding her feelings, she needed to tell Jago exactly how she felt—he couldn't read her mind. Honesty was always cleaner and led to fewer misunderstandings.

'Yes, I want you to mean it,' she replied. 'Did you?'

He sent her a tender smile. 'Very much so.'

Relief washed over her. 'Good,' she told him, with a huge smile. 'Because I still want a decent proposal—nothing too over-the-top—and a kick-ass ring. And we are getting married in a church, by a priest, Le Roux, and I sure as hell want a honeymoon.'

Jago cupped his hand behind her head and bridged the gap between them. 'Proposal, ring, church wedding, honeymoon… I'm taking mental notes. Anything else, my darling?'

Dodi's hand snuck up and under his shirt, revelling in the feel of his hot skin, his hard muscles. 'Just for you to love me, Jago, every day and in every way.'

'I do, I will, Elodie Kate. That's a promise.'

Jago dropped his head to kiss her, but before he could, Dodi took his hand and placed it on her small bump. 'We're a family, Jago. *Finally.*'

He kissed the corner of her mouth. 'That we are. And you are, and always will be, the centre of our world.'

* * * * *

Loved The Billionaire's One-Night Baby?
Don't miss the next installments in the Scandals of the Le Roux Wedding trilogy, coming soon.

In the meantime, make sure to dive into these other Joss Wood stories!

How to Undo the Proud Billionaire
How to Win the Wild Billionaire
How to Tempt the Off-Limits Billionaire
The Rules of Their Red-Hot Reunion

Available now!

COMING NEXT MONTH FROM

HARLEQUIN

PRESENTS

#4017 A BABY TO TAME THE WOLFE

Passionately Ever After...

by Heidi Rice

Billionaire Jack Wolfe is ruthless, arrogant...yet so infuriatingly attractive that Katherine spends a scorching night with him! After their out-of-this-world encounter, she never expected his convenient proposal or her response, "I'm pregnant..."

#4018 STOLEN NIGHTS WITH THE KING

Passionately Ever After...

by Sharon Kendrick

King Corso's demand that innocent Rosie accompany him on an international royal tour can't be denied. Neither can their forbidden passion! They know it can only be temporary. But as time runs out, will their stolen nights be enough?

#4019 THE KISS SHE CLAIMED FROM THE GREEK

Passionately Ever After...

by Abby Green

One kiss. That's all innocent Sofie intends to steal from the gorgeous sleeping stranger. But her moment of complete irrationality wakes billionaire Achilles up! And awakens in her a longing she's never experienced...

#4020 A SCANDAL MADE AT MIDNIGHT

Passionately Ever After...

by Kate Hewitt

CEO Alessandro's brand needs an image overhaul and he's found the perfect influencer to court. Only, it's her plain older stepsister, Liane, whom he can't stop thinking about! Risking the scandal of a sizzling fling may be worth it for a taste of the fairy tale...

HPCNMRA0522

#4021 CINDERELLA IN THE BILLIONAIRE'S CASTLE

Passionately Ever After...

by Clare Connelly

Tormented by the guilt of his past, superrich recluse Thirio has deprived himself of the wild pleasures he once craved. Until Lucinda makes it past the imposing, steel-reinforced doors of his Alpine castle. And now he craves one forbidden night...with her!

#4022 THE PRINCESS HE MUST MARRY

Passionately Ever After...

by Jadesola James

Spare heir Prince Akil's plan is simple: conveniently wed Princess Tobi, gain his inheritance and escape the prison of his royal life. Then they'll go their separate ways. It's going well. Until he finds himself indisputably attracted to his innocent new bride!

#4023 UNDONE BY HER ULTRA-RICH BOSS

Passionately Ever After...

by Lucy King

Exhausted after readying Duarte's Portuguese vineyard for an event, high-end concierge Orla falls asleep between his luxurious sheets. He's clearly unimpressed—but also so ridiculously sexy that she knows the heat between them will be uncontainable...

#4024 HER SECRET ROYAL DILEMMA

Passionately Ever After...

by Chantelle Shaw

After Arielle saved Prince Eirik from drowning, their attraction was instant! Now Arielle faces the ultimate dilemma: indulge in their rare, irresistible connection, knowing her shocking past could taint his royal future...or walk away?

SPECIAL EXCERPT FROM

HARLEQUIN

PRESENTS

Tormented by the guilt of his past, superrich recluse Thirio has deprived himself of the wild pleasures he once craved. Until Lucinda makes it past the imposing, steel-reinforced doors of his Alpine castle. And now he craves one forbidden night...with her!

Read on for a sneak preview of Clare Connelly's next story for Harlequin Presents Cinderella in the Billionaire's Castle.

"You cannot leave."

"Why not?"

"The storm will be here within minutes." As if nature wanted to underscore his point, another bolt of lightning split the sky in two; a crack of thunder followed. "You won't make it down the mountain."

Lucinda's eyes slashed to the gates that led to the castle, and beyond them, the narrow road that had brought her here. Even in the sunshine of the morning, the drive had been somewhat hair-raising. She didn't relish the prospect of skiing her way back down to civilization.

She turned to look at him, but that was a mistake, because his chest was at eye height, and she wanted to stare and lose herself in the details she saw there, the story behind his scar, the sculpted nature of his muscles. Compelling was an understatement.

HPEXP0522

"So what do you suggest?" she asked carefully.

"There's only one option." The words were laced with displeasure. "You'll have to spend the night here."

"Spend the night," she repeated breathily. "Here. With you?"

"Not with me, no. But in my home, yes."

"I'm sure I'll be fine to drive."

"Will you?" Apparently, Thirio saw through her claim. "Then go ahead." He took a step backward, yet his eyes remained on her face, and for some reason, it almost felt to Lucinda as though he were touching her.

Rain began to fall, icy and hard. Lucinda shivered.

"I— You're right," she conceded after a beat. "Are you sure it's no trouble?"

"I didn't say that."

"Maybe the storm will clear quickly."

"Perhaps by morning."

"Perhaps?"

"Who knows."

The prospect of being marooned in this incredible castle with this man for any longer than one night loomed before her. Anticipation hummed in her veins.

HPEXP0522

The Perfect Fake Date
NAIMA SIMONE
One Little Secret
MAUREEN CHILD
FREE
Value Over
$20
Presents
Melanie Milburne
The Temporary Mrs. Marchetti
Presents
Amanda Cinelli
The Secret to Marrying Marchesi